ADVANCED OUTDOOR LEARNING

Creating a Whole-School Culture

Craig Taylor

First published in the United Kingdom 2012

Attitude Matters Publications
Frome
Somerset

www.attitudematters.org

Copyright © 2012 Craig Taylor

All rights reserved. This book may not be reproduced in whole or in part, stored in a retrieval system or transmitted in any form or by any means without the prior permission of the copyright owner.

The right of Craig Taylor to be identified as the author has been asserted by him in accordance with the Copyright, Designs and Patents Act 1988.

A catalogue record for this book is available from the British Library.

ISBN 978-1-291-03391-5

DEDICATION

To my mother, Lois Taylor, whose life-time of teaching set the foundations for my own and whose words and advice I turned to so often, both in the classroom and out.

Contents

Culture is the Key ... 1
1. Like the heart ... 3
2. Whole-school Culture ... 5
3. Something In It for Us? ... 8

Outdoor Learning Graveyards ... 13
4. Where Are We Now? ... 16
5. Research Papers, Studies & Reports ... 18

Play is Just the Beginning ... 25
6. Are You Sure That's Really a Den? ... 28
7. Metaphor & Imagination ... 33
8. Who's Watching? ... 35

Getting Your Hands Dirty ... 40
9. Outdoor Learning is *Not* a Subject ... 41
10. Verticality, Horizontality, Embedding ... 44
11. Play/Work ... 45
12. Diversions & Dead-Ends ... 49

The Nuts & Bolts ... 55
Step 1: Connections ... 55
Step 2: Evidence ... 56
Step 3: When & Where? ... 57
Step 4: Processes ... 57
Step 5: Policy ... 59
Step 6: How & Why? ... 60

It's Never What to Teach; It's *How* to Teach — 62

13. Whose Discipline? — 62
14. Confidence & Engagement — 66
15. Resource 'Junkies' — 78

The Vertical & Horizontal Axes — 80

16. Planning for Embedded Verticality — 80
17. Topics & Projects — 83
18. Linking Back – Content Threads — 84
19. The Four Keys & the Horizontal Axis — 87
    - Key 1: Level — 88
    - Key 2: Order — 92
    - Key 3: System — 96
    - Key 4: Closure — 97

Four Whole-School Elements — 99

20. Element 1: Children — 99
21. Element 2: Home — 103
22. Element 3: Nature — 110
23. Element 4: Teachers — 118

Wrapping Up — 122

Appendices — 128

Example Outdoor Learning Policy — 128
Outdoor Classrooms: A Growing Convention — 137
Online Research Sources — 141
Publications & Research Documents — 142

Culture is the Key

All I did was to leave the tap running. The rest was simply a matter of riding the wave that followed.

Early summer, heading towards Christmas and the long holidays, last term of the year – a dry, Mediterranean climate in southern Australia - and the children, by mid-afternoon, were hot and bothered, hanging around the outside tap. How many times a day we teachers asked them, *told* them, not to flick water at each other, pour drinking bottles down friends' necks and then over their own heads, I don't know. But the tap had quickly become a central gathering point during those hot afternoons - filling bottles, wetting hands and shrieking at each glorious moment of cold shock as drops splashed onto dry skin under the sun.

It seemed to me at the time that like just about everything of genuine value that I created as a teacher, this was another of those wonderful experiences which, of course I didn't create at all; I simply noticed something happening, captured it in the moment and found ways to encourage it to grow.

This particular experience occurred early on in my career and became enormously important in how I came to see teaching in its widest and deepest sense. It

set the first foundation stones in place for my understanding of real engagement and the nature of experience in that process.

Most of our classrooms were single dwellings, bordered by verandas and sited a little distance apart from the next building and year group. The tap was attached to the veranda post of the neighbouring classroom and a wide, dusty path lay between the two buildings. Down the contours on the path and along the foot-traffic markings in the dirt, the water now flowed, escaping the many containers held out by the children, splashing its way freely downhill.

The 'flood' began in a large and ever growing puddle directly beneath the tap, finishing in a tiny wave of mud and dust, which trickled towards the playground beyond. By the time it had created the beginnings of a rivulet in the dirt, children were flocking to its growing banks, damming up the walls with whatever they could scrape into 'defences' and shouting gleefully to each other to get to work.

As I watched that hugely creative moment unfold in those first few minutes, I began to see a myriad of threads and levels of creative involvement in the children's play. It was as if I grasped as a young teacher, in that moment for the first time, the real significance of what they were doing together. I could see the potentials for expansion, the connection between what was happening in front of me and other play experiences and I knew I had begun to understand why the children called this their *work*.

Like the Heart

There is no instinct like the heart.
Lord Byron

I have been working with and teaching outdoor learning for over 30 years. I am not an outdoor education instructor though; I am a teacher. I don't train children in how to use climbing ropes, how to cave, sail, hike, camp out, ride horses, mountain bikes or even camels! My field of work is not outdoor adventure. I am a primary school teacher. My fields are children and education.

Because I have always sought how best to engage children in their learning, I have spent as much time as I could, creating and providing experience-based learning opportunities for them. Of course this very often took us outdoors. But I approach outdoor learning from the perspective of a teacher first and foremost. The reason I take children outdoors is not because the forest, the stream or the desert hills need us. It's because we need them.

I have been particularly lucky to have worked in a wide range of school settings across the sectors in state, independent and alternative schools and in different countries as well as in the different systems. But I was especially lucky as a young teacher, to have been encouraged to follow my instincts and use the outdoors with children whenever I was able. I continued as I began. I found my way by watching children's experiences and seeing what worked. Over time, I learned how to expand and progress their successes and gradually gained a firmer grasp of how to create the conditions for that learning to flourish.

So now, one of the key areas of what I do is to inspire teachers and help schools develop the confidence, imagination and insight to work with the outdoors themselves – one of the most direct and worthwhile ways available to us as teachers to engage children most fully in their learning.

Children will devote themselves to their 'work' and to the process of their learning if only given the chance to do so. But we teachers have to find a way to connect and reconnect them to this process. For some, it means having to unlock a way which seems blocked and unresponsive. For many, engaging fully and openly in their learning is becoming more and more challenging. To give children the chance to discover this level of work, where they can identify with the activity as their own and throw themselves into the task without barriers, we have to understand and be able to bring about real *engagement learning*. Working experientially with children outdoors is central to this process.

Advanced Outdoor Learning: A Whole School Culture focuses on some of the most important elements I have learned in these 30 years for how to deliver genuine outdoor learning. But at the outset we need to underline very clearly, that what we are looking to achieve in our schools and for our children is not actually a focus on *outdoor* learning after all. It is a focus on learning itself - in all its breadth and forms.

Outdoor learning like all other aspects of teaching and learning, needs to be a vehicle for what we are trying to accomplish for our children overall – real progress in the whole of their education – but real progress, not just in accumulating information – real progress for the head and for the heart.

Whole-School Culture

Developing a whole-school culture is a key, not only to healthy and sustainable *outdoor* learning and teaching. It is a key to healthy and sustainable learning and teaching altogether.

Whenever I walk up to a school's gates I always have the feeling that I am entering a special place. Shouting and laughter spill over the walls from the playground. A flash of colour and the squeals of the chase as someone runs past the gates hint at the life and vibrancy beyond. Even from the car park, it seems there is a sense of this something special in the air – welcoming, unsure, cosy, open, concerned, interested, calm – just the beginning of a sense of it.

Of course, it's much more complex than that – and after meeting teachers, parents, seeing children, working with staff – that first impression is overrun and rolled into countless moments that make up my image of the school. Later, when it's time to leave and I have a chance to reflect, it's always interesting how a thread seems to appear. Starting from that very first impression, there is a suggestion of the school as a whole, of its nature, a hint of something special in the life of this particular school - of its identity and the culture that flows through it.

A culture is a shared experience. It is the combined school community engagement and it suggests an ethos, an attitude which people recognise as an essential part of the school. In fact this culture is an indication of the character of the school itself - and because a school is somehow more than the sum of its many, many parts, this 'hard-to-put-your-finger-on' aspect of its identity is dependent on the actual experience of those who make up the school community.

Together, the total community creates the constantly changing, growing and evolving life and culture of the school - parents, teachers, children, school leaders and the wider local community - all the way through to supporting government departments.

The culture has a tone, something which others recognise from a distance. They see it in the way the children interact with others. They hear it through parents' stories. Where it is progressive, engaging and constructive, they notice a level of positive activity which seems to have a 'buzz' about it. Everyone experiences it, responding to it in one way or another.

Children, parents and teachers are particularly influenced. It engages and encourages them and draws them into a like-minded sense of belonging, of being a part of something moving forward.

Many factors influence the nature of this culture, its strength, clarity and inclusiveness. The quality of the head teacher's leadership is especially important. The specific constellation of parents and families involved in the school at any one time has a large impact and the complex inter-relationships that evolve in such a crucially linked social group can shape the success of the school's efforts. Their positivity and support gives the developing culture a sense of affirmation and approval.

Teachers' enthusiasm and motivation are critical. Their influence passes down through the children and on to the parents. When staff members are positive and clear about what the school is trying to achieve and how to accomplish those shared goals, they lead 'from the front.' Their commitment is an essential part of the culture itself and of continuing to define its character.

Teachers want to teach. They want to see the children in their classes being successful, progressing and happy. They want to feel a part of something good. This is what moves them to become teachers in the first place. A teacher at the top of h/er game creates a 'hum' in the class of constructive, creative activity. There is a sense of discovery, of joy in the learning and, regardless of the age group, of work. This is the same 'hum' school leaders need to engender in their staff. It takes a good deal of effort and care from everyone involved, but when it exists, it inspires the whole of the community.

Parents in particular, notice changes in their children's motivation. Enthusiastic children tend to talk about what they are doing and want to share it with others. This is one of the outcomes schools notice when they take their classes outside. Many of the children, whose normal answer to their parents' stock questions at pick-up time - 'How was school today? What did you do?' is, 'OK. Nothing,' - very often find they have something else to say.

A whole-school culture is a culture of engagement. We bring about a greater community school spirit when parents and teachers recognise changes in the children's excitement and interest. Their enthusiasm carries the school forward and this in turn, encourages greater positive involvement by all. The tone changes.It becomes inclusive, communicative, and active and the school is identified as a great place to be, a great school to be part of.

Something In It for Us?

Outdoor learning offers something significant for teachers and for the way they work as well as it does for children. But it is not simply a matter of rushing outside. I have seen it many times, where a teacher takes the class out and after half an hour it is clear that it would have been better for all to have stayed inside. No amount of fresh air can really make up for a class, either in chaos on the one hand or controlled by boring and rigid box-ticking on the other.

There must be a 'method in the madness,' and learning how to work constructively outdoors with children gives a real opportunity for practical, evidence-based professional development. Lessons learned in this process will flow over into the rest of our teaching.

If we want to focus and direct children's engagement outdoors constructively, it means that we will need to adjust our teaching and our teaching methods to a way of learning which may not be at all familiar, especially not when our training has had a very different emphasis. For some this will certainly mean more modification than for others. It means learning how to use children's natural tendencies for play, exploration and discovery. And in particular, it means learning how to prepare for these experiences, how to follow them up and then how consolidate what has been learned.

At the present stage in the development of outdoor learning as a part of teaching in primary schools, there is a very clear area of need: *knowing how to maintain momentum by ordering and extending children's responses to their experiences.* These two closely linked aspects offer real potential for the improvement of delivery:

Programmes need to offer longer and more sustained outdoor experiences.

These programmes need to be characterised by well-designed preparatory and follow-up work.

Rickinson (2004)

The initiative for these changes needs to be taken by teachers, with school leadership support. It requires re-thinking how to develop a methodology and along with this, understanding how to sustain the changes as best practice.

The challenge is that in order for a methodology like this to really deliver the claims made for it, teachers need to be imaginative and creative as well as being organised and thorough. But we cannot suddenly expect our teachers to be imaginative. Nor can we force them to be creative. Never-the-less, I am always amazed at how readily they begin to show exactly these qualities when working with me outdoors as part of further training and are given the encouragement and opportunity to rediscover that part of themselves.

'I've got a really crooked head.'

'Yes, my arms are way too long. And look at my legs. I'll never be able to stand up.'

One of the exercises I have teachers try is to make little figures out of mud. Take a garden spade and a watering can and begin to dig up a little of the school yard. Pour in some water and then reach down to take out some of the forming mud.

It couldn't be simpler. While I'm speaking to the teachers about play and children's work, I'll fashion a primitive, hand-held figure from the mud, usually nothing more than a squeezed ball, separating a suggested head from the body. Then I'll have them make one of their own.

Occasionally someone will be concerned about getting their hands dirty, but more often, the first task is to stop them talking amongst themselves, deflecting attention, making jokes and distracting their colleagues. These are, of course, behaviours we recognise quickly in children, but not nearly as easily in ourselves!

Then I'll suggest looking about for bits of stick, leaves and so on to add to the figure. As they search about on the school yard floor, each hunting for that 'perfect' twig they know is out there, the conversations quieten and a 'working hum' begins. That is when they begin to speak about the little mud figure in the first person.

'I've got a really big nose now.'

Whenever we are being creative, we identify with whatever we 'create' as a first person experience. It is an incredibly intimate feeling and we have it from early on in our lives. As we grow older and our sense of self-consciousness becomes more and more intense, being 'creative' can be difficult and exposing. Without encouragement and common sense support, most people stop doing anything they think of as creative or 'arty' in favour of activities that feel safer and less personally challenging. We tend to define ourselves as being in one or other of two groups – good at or *not* good at 'art.'

So it's not unexpected to see some teachers acting out the 'naughty child' at the beginning of the process, unconsciously trying to reduce the stress they feel being asked to make anything in public. It is always encouraging however, to see how quickly they throw that inhibition off and dive in, once they recognise how deeply connected the task is to the nature of children and children's creative work.

Right from the outset it is important to note that creating a whole-school outdoor learning culture provides real learning opportunities for all the groups in the school community. It is not something the teachers simply do for the children. It is as much for their professional and personal development as it is for anyone else. We teach children the process even more than we teach them the content. Teaching high quality outdoor learning requires an organised structure and a clear eye on the method of delivery. But at the heart of the process is the teacher's own imagination and creativity. Everyone is, *by nature* creative and imaginative and this process needs us as teachers, to be prepared to rediscover that capacity which we may well have rejected early in our own school lives.

Outdoor Learning Graveyards

Things are changing for outdoor learning in the UK. The first flush of enthusiasm for getting children outdoors, both by teachers and parents has passed. This came after, or at least, coincided with the 'Let Our Children Play' 10th September 2007 letter in the Telegraph, signed by 270 leading lights in the field, dedicated to children and education.

It followed two alarming reports: Britain's children, according to UNICEF were amongst the unhappiest in the developed world and the children's charity NPC had pointed to an explosion in children's clinically diagnosable mental health problems contributing to their discontent.

A main cause of this disturbing condition they believed to be, *'the marked decline over the last 15 years in children's play– particularly outdoor, unstructured, loosely supervised play, vital to children's all-round health and well-being.'*

Around the same time the Learning Outside the Classroom (LOtC) manifesto was published, stating:

'We believe that every young person should experience the world beyond the classroom as an essential part of learning and personal development.'

Genuine support for outdoor learning: reduction in red tape, revision of Health & Safety concerns and a redirection of priorities, all encouraged teachers who loved the natural world to take their classes outside. Forest School emerged as a brand and a host of often government funded organisations sprang into being, looking for new ways of promoting to schools.

Teachers, with the best will in the world, rushed into their school grounds to erect bug hotels and hang dream-catchers in whatever trees they could find. Builders recognised an opportunity to sell gazebos in the guise of 'outdoor classrooms.' Parents rallied to raise funds, wanting to have the next 'must-have' in the playground. A school pond became essential. Insects were rebranded and repackaged as mini-beasts and thousands of children went on 'bear hunts.'

Once you show a particular interest in an area like this, especially when head teachers are being asked from above what their outdoor learning policy is, it's only a matter of time before you then have to organise a lot more than your own lessons!

Enter the world of internet based resources - a rich menu of hundreds of outdoor possibilities at your fingertips - much of it more 'busy work' involving plastic pots, discarded tyres and bits of paper on sticks. Finding time to plan, let alone to be imaginative can be a challenge and so we are often drawn to the easy 'resource finder' solution.

Add our enthusiastic gardener to the potential for creating a mixture of mud and plastic litter in the school grounds and you get the classic outdoor learning 'graveyard.'

Many primary schools have these 'graveyards' of well-intentioned initiatives scattered throughout their school grounds – half-finished projects, abandoned pallet box 'bug hotels', willow tangles, planter pots, string and even tools scattered about, wool and paper 'sculptures' and 'catchers' hanging in the trees - the list goes on!

I have seen dozens of schools over the last couple of years who have passed through this first phase - filling their grounds with 'stuff' - stuff which is not allowed to be cleared away because it's a child's creation, an outdoor learning treasure. The end of this phase is often characterised by the enthusiastic pioneer, who led the first movement into outdoor learning leaving the school for greener pastures.

The Early Years teachers have very often developed quite a lot of outdoor learning experience by this stage and as children are coming into the older years, both they and their parents notice that there is a discrepancy between what is now being offered compared to what went on when the children were younger. Concerns about the difficulties of engaging boys, particularly in literacy programmes have highlighted the fact that outdoor work may better suit many of them, supporting their progress in other areas.

There is pressure to 'keep up.' The question is, how best to manage it, with the normal competition for resources, time and attention that schools have to balance.

Where Are We Now?

Many schools have someone new in post who has been asked to oversee outdoor learning in the school. They have a bit of a 'graveyard' in the grounds. The rest of the staff may well be a little cynical, if not resistant after the initial wave of eagerness. Time races on. Seasonal change is always on its way, bringing with it the ever-present problems of appropriate clothing and wet weather concerns. And then there is the sense of limbo head teachers and their staff endure each time they await potential changes to the government expectations of what to teach and how they are to teach it.

Furthermore, the latest research into children's well-being has certainly not improved. Groups promoting children and nature have continued to work hard to influence policy around the world, making considerable gains, and there is a mounting body of up-to-date research in support of the benefits of connection to nature and outdoor experiences for children.

As a result of this, there are now large, funded projects looking at the best ways of incorporating outdoor learning in schools. This leads understandably, to questions about whether there have been any of the benefits promised so far by school-based outdoor learning and it's important to be able to distinguish these from other forms of nature experience. And of course, it raises the question of what we are to do and how we are to do it, if we really do want outdoor learning in our schools to play a constructive part in the children and nature movement.

The 'graveyard' is a typical symptom of there *not* being a pervading culture of outdoor learning in the school. Even though there may have been the best of intentions, honest enthusiasm on the part of some teachers and parents, great enthusiasm on the part of the children and even strong support by the head teacher, outdoor experiences:

Have tended to remain relatively isolated occurrences that are few and far between.

Are concentrated in the early years, dwindling towards the older classes.

Are not followed up through the years in an evolving progression.

An authentic outdoor learning culture means that spending time outdoors in constructive learning situations, using the outdoors creatively and developing an on-going and maturing outdoor relationship for the children, comes as second nature to the teachers in the school.

It means that the outdoors is seen by the teachers as a source of imagination, of inspiration for *their own work*. They recognise that it is essential for their own creative teaching and a foundation for the children's genuine engagement in learning.

The rest of the culture – the support for developing the school's outdoor landscape, a focus on a rich and integrated curriculum, the interest by parents to encourage and be involved and so on *will grow around this one key aspect* – the strength of the teachers' commitment to their own creative work.

Research Papers, Studies & Reports

There has been a huge amount of interest worldwide in children and nature and as a result, in outdoor learning. This has led to a great deal of research in the field to establish the links between playing and working in nature and the outcomes of those on-going experiences. Although many take it as given that children can only benefit from what they see as a more 'natural' approach to learning, there are challenges to the view, especially in terms of the role schools can and should be playing.

I have included several of the best sources for research documents below. Reviews of the research provide an overview of the findings and although it is more than likely that not all claims will stand up in their present form to further scrutiny, the general consensus is that the body of evidence supports the view that children benefit enormously from their engagement with nature.

Moreover, there is also clear evidence to indicate the contrary position is also true: that children, whose experience of nature is very restricted and who do not form an engagement with the environment are likely to suffer for that lack.

'For many paediatricians, the strategic paediatric priorities have changed from infectious disease, immunizations and car seats and helmets to mental health, obesity and early brain development, all of which could be changed by re-connecting our kids to the wonder of nature.' Dr Mary Brown, American Academy of Paediatrics

Richard Louv's book *'Last Child in the Woods,'* has formed the basis for a hugely popular movement around the world in support of nature's constructive role for children. He proposed the term 'nature deficit disorder' as an attempt to express what his research had indicated, that children need to have a nature experience and that when they do not, a range of predictable problems is likely to arise.

It is another step to suggest that outdoor learning or learning in the natural environments (LINE) also provides similar benefits. Some may well worry about the idea that, with all the pressures primary schools have on the amount of time there is in the school day and the demands of delivering key curriculum subjects, outdoor learning is something they should even be considering, let alone taking on as a responsibility.

Regardless of the demonstrable benefits when children are reconnected with nature and certainly reconnected with hands-on, tactile experience as opposed to virtual experience, if we are looking at making outdoor learning a key part of primary school education, we need to be very clear that it provides solutions, not more problems.

It is a common occurrence for head teachers to bemoan the fact that their teachers are not taking up the outdoor learning opportunities available to them after having had an introduction to the possibilities.

'It's a beautiful day outside. I've just been walking around the grounds. There's not a single class out there. What a waste. So much to do and no one doing it!' is a typical comment I hear from heads. There is just too much for those teachers to do and too much inertia in managing what they are already doing, to allow any time to explore something new. At least that is often the perception. We need very good reasons to expect a serious change.

Dillon and Dickie (2012) point out in their review of the social and economic benefits, specifically in relation to schools and LINE, that alongside the 'traditional challenges facing schools' as reported by teachers, of 'fear of accident, cost and curriculum pressures,' there are also those of poor teacher confidence, concerns over self-efficacy and a lack of access to appropriate training.

'Importantly these local challenges appear to underpin, and hence are more significant than those traditionally cited by schools and providers.'

What does the evidence suggest?

Being near nature, perhaps only having a view of nature can help to reduce stress in children.

If older children spend more time outdoors, they are usually more physically active and less likely to be overweight than those children spending more time indoors. (We know less about very young children in this respect.)

Children who live in 'greener' areas appear to have more stable body weight changes.

Myopia may be helped by spending time outdoors.

Green exercise appears to add benefits not achieved by equal exertion in 'normal' gyms.

Children, and their families are helped if hospitals, and medical clinics incorporate nature into their designs, reducing stress and improving the healing process.

Most adult care-givers, parents and guardians prefer the idea of 'play,' and nature play than 'exercise.'

Pupils, who are involved in school environmental learning programmes often do better on standardized tests.

Children find it easier to concentrate after spending time in nature. Their attention is more focused.

Children's creativity is enhanced by playing in natural environments.

Being involved with nature supports children's self-discipline and self-confidence, including children with disabilities.

Natural environments aid recovery from mental tiredness, helping the process of learning for children.

Natural environments offer hands-on, multi-sensory stimulation. This is ideal for early childhood brain development.

Children's play is more sharing, with less conflict when they are in natural environments.

Playing in natural areas supports children who have been diagnosed with attention-deficit/hyperactivity disorder (ADHD) or attention-deficit disorder (ADD.) and seems to significantly reduce symptoms for children as young as five.

See, for example:

Dillon, J. & Dickie, I. (2012) 'Understanding the diverse benefits of learning in natural environments' in *Learning in the Natural Environment: Review of social and economic benefits and barriers*

Louv, R (2010) 'Grow Outside' *Keynote address to the American Academy of Pediatrics National Conference, October 2, San Francisco*

The Children's Nature Institute, Los Angeles, USA: *www.childrensnatureinstitute.org*

In the cited review, (above) the authors (2012) note that the research offers a *'diverse and compelling'* case for LINE in schools and as part of school practice. The fact is however, that many different types of learning experience are being gathered together under broad umbrellas. LOtC (Learning Outside the Classroom) includes everything from a visit to the local museum, a play, an off-site, residential adventure week as well as activities which are included in natural environment learning. There will be similarities in understanding and managing the different types of activity, for example its capacity for being memorable, although I seemed to recall, as a child, a lot more about the bus journey than the actual Roman 'whatsits.'

There is quite a jump from recognising a children-nature connection to supporting a clear policy intention such as:

'Natural Connections', (for Natural England) objectives are to - stimulate the demand from schools and teachers for learning outside the classroom in natural environments.' Rickinson (2012)

One wonders which is being driven first, the horse or the cart and is it just because this is where we find children gathered in large groups, that schools are being expected to remedy what is clearly a much wider and deeper social problem?

Never-the-less, Dillon *et al* do offer a very useful analysis of the research, divided into the following areas:

Increasing knowledge and understanding

Developing skills

Changing attitudes and behaviours

Health and well-being benefits

Self-efficacy and self-worth

Benefits to schools, teachers and the wider community

Benefits to the natural environment

Perhaps the most important point they make is included almost as rider, that although 'substantial evidence' does exist, the success of outdoor learning experiences is dependent on them being,

'...properly conceived, adequately planned, well taught and effectively followed up.'

This simple sentence, tripping easily off the tongue has a particularly wide reach however. It sets out a challenge which was first highlighted by Rickinson (2004). In over eight years then, the problem still remains. How do you *actually* teach outdoor learning to achieve its best?

24

Play is Just the Beginning

School-based outdoor learning is in many ways a wonderfully simple combination of two essentials for a child's well-being - learning through experience and building a direct and intimate relationship with nature. Both elements come naturally to children given the right opportunities.

When a young child is involved in learning through experience, we generally describe it as a form of play and as a natural and spontaneous expression; it is a key indicator of a child's relationship with the world around. From both research and the understanding of practitioners worldwide in the field of education and child development, it has become clear however, that the depth and extent of children's play have been changing. This seems to be very much as a result of social and economic factors and particularly with changes in available technology.

I certainly notice more and more children at a loss to know quite what to do with themselves when they are outdoors unless there are white lines and goal posts or obvious pieces of play equipment for them to use. Their interaction with a natural environment can be far more challenging; especially if it is something they are not accustomed to being in.

Interestingly, I have had many children on courses in the forest who actually live in leafy, wooded areas, who walk the dog with their mothers along forest paths and who know all about 'the countryside' and who never-the-less show the same unease in the natural setting The first thing many of them ask to do is to make a 'den.' It is very common however, for them to be squabbling after a very short time about nothing in particular, without having reached first base in their building.

They try to balance large boughs on unsteady saplings, can't picture how to create a space under a log or heap up a roof made of branches and leaves. They haven't either the patience to persist with the task nor the experience to know what will work and what won't - and so they often end up with nothing but the frustrated feeling that they had wanted to do something but weren't really sure what they were trying to do anyway.

Although they are familiar, to some extent with the natural environment, they are not familiar with play, certainly not constructive, imaginative play and so their interaction with their surroundings has not been nearly as deep as it might have been. They try to engage in ways we would expect for their age, almost as an unconscious drive, but they cannot prolong the activity or find a full expression of it.

A child's play changes over time but like all behaviours, play evolves rather than simply changes. We see vertical patterns appearing through children's early lives and on into and then beyond adolescence.

Many of the elements from early childhood play continue to be evident as they grow older. Although they evolve over time, we can still recognise the development as maturing strands, even when the behaviours appear no longer to be similar on the surface.

The way these different elements mature is very important for the healthy nature of the growing child's relationship to self, others and the environment. Early years' play serves as a foundation. If a young child cannot fully express him/herself through play, the ability, as an older child to do so in more sophisticated forms of interaction is restricted. The verticality is a measure of connectedness.

We know for example, that a child's struggle with language development impacts on their capacity for communication in *all its forms*. We also know that this early struggle becomes the root of challenges in later life, which can then be very difficult, if at all possible to overcome.

We see the same connectedness in the development of play. An evolving behaviour builds what can appear to be a new form of expression on its earlier foundations. It is critical to be able to see how these behaviours are part of an emerging continuum. Although self-evident when put like this, it is amazing how unrecognised it is, even by teachers, whose work it is to understand and notice developmental changes and links.

Are You Sure That's a Den?

Some time ago I was preparing an outdoor learning training day for a primary school in the country. I had visited the school to explore and assess the grounds, meet the head teacher, discuss what they were doing and hoping to achieve with the day for the teachers. I was particularly impressed with the head's vision for change in her school and also with the neat and tidy nature of each of the class rooms.

On our walk around the grounds, however, I couldn't find anywhere where there was any bare soil. I needed a place to work with a small group of teachers, so it only needed to be an area a couple of yards across.

The whole of the children's playing area was either covered in tarmac or sealed over with a rubber substance, which even had little rubber leaves and sticks glued to the surface. Someone had sold the school a classic health and safety driven solution!

As I drove away from the school, I noticed a small copse of wood only a couple of hundreds yard from the school gate. I thought this might be possible to use. When I returned for another school preparation visit, I thought I might explore the wood but noticed a small group of teenage boys heading for the stile entrance amongst the trees.

I turned the car around, only too aware that I had best not make my way into the wood right then, only to find they

28

had placed a look-out, the youngest of the group, nonchalantly lounging on his bike at the stile. Now I was very curious. I slowed and tried to peer into the dark copse through the trees as I glided by. The look-out was very agitated at this! All of a sudden I noticed a couple of bare torsos moving about in the thicket. At this point I knew I was definitely not going in there and quickly accelerated away.

The next morning, before the start of the training day, I stopped at the copse to see what I could find. Of course at 7.00am there were not likely to be any teenagers about, probably not even awake! A narrow path led into the wood, occasional, broken boughs along the way. Inside there was an open space, the size of a large room, with paths leading off into the surrounding trees. Some litter and wooden boards lay about the floor, which was uneven, heaped up into mounds and ridden into a myriad of small tracks. I had stumbled into a young teenagers' den – a bike track, hidden away and lawless – the perfect getaway for the local, fresh adolescents – and with all the hallmarks of a typical den, found the world over, distinguished by characteristic elements regardless of the age of the builders and occupiers.

Den building is a useful example to take, highlighting the way a strand of play activity can develop over time. We are all aware of it as typical healthy outdoor and indoor play. But we may not be as familiar with the social and psychological aspects. Children begin very early to create a small division between themselves and others. Even the game of 'boo!' – in which a child hides and then reappears, first behind hands and then the cushion, the sofa and so on - is a developing element of this play motif.

The play distinguishes me from you, but in the first instance, inside from outside, my place from your place.

When they come to 'build' their first dens, the construction may simply be a small wall of blocks or a space behind a chair, the 'roof' and technical parts coming later. A cloth or leafy twig may be all that is needed to suggest a roof because the entire experience is largely held within the child's imagination. The roof, the walls are aspects of establishing my place or my home and separating it from the outside. It encourages and nurtures hugely important feelings of safety and protection. A child's sense of security is enhanced by their expressive, imaginative play.

As they grow older the dens become more complex, more sophisticated, depending on their builder's level of technical ability and experience. Eventually shelters, forts and dens are constructed which may even have rooms, be waterproof and act as semi-permanent huts. The classic tree house is typical of this level of sophistication, often requiring the use of tools, fixings and dressed timber, along with covering materials such as board and tin sheeting.

But alongside the actual building and constructing activity there is the extremely important story or narrative that is being played out. Younger children will express the story out loud, changing it amongst themselves as they need according to the play. They may begin by imitating what they know as household tasks in a fantasy room using fantasy crockery, furniture and eating fantasy food.

Playing *in* the den is a phase deeper in the play than *building* the den. In situations where children have been able to build dens which are not cleared away and which do fulfil the innate drive they have to create this space away from the adult world, the play *in* the den takes many forms. It metamorphoses, passing through different imaginative narratives, often combined with rebuilding, rearranging and adding to the den. But what is important is that the den is no longer a pile of sticks. It becomes much more than a construction. It begins to have a life of its own, animated by the children's play and reflecting their psychology.

The den is a living, growing art form, allowing the children to express their instincts, practise and rehearse social dynamics and where they can begin to form an uninhibited sense of self – all in the quiet and security of *their place*, in the secret of the wild.

Key points:

Outdoor play develops as an evolving strand.

The roots of the play, in the early years are critical to continuing healthy play development.

The play has a *psychological content* which is crucial for the children to explore, rehearse and progress in an uninhibited, creative environment.

What we learn first, as young children through our 'play-relationships,' forms the foundations of the way we continue to experience and explore the world around us as we grow older.

When we understand the developmental aspects of a child's learning and engage their natural inclinations for play, discovery and creativity, we can create far deeper learning opportunities. Evolving play is not entirely linear however. We have the remarkable ability to learn from different and sometimes seemingly unconnected experiences. The imaginative, fantasy world of the young child brings everything into a whole, a connectedness, where there are no differentiations between what can and cannot be, where the world opens and expands to be anything, anytime and anywhere.

The connections are creative and artistic. Realities are blurred and representation becomes a foundation of the way a child builds associations and interrelationships.

'This is a spoon,' states the child, holding up a stick.

'I need a knife though,' replies her friend.

'Yes, this is a knife,' the first child answers, passing her the same stick.

These children are *inside their play*. They are in an imaginative world which they are building, creating and modifying as the narrative unfolds. It is both play and *a play*.

Metaphor & the Imagination

Cultural expression depends on the communication of deep experience through metaphor. Artists explore the potentials within representations as a way of evoking rich, layered responses. Our ability to connect to their language and images with depth relies on prior experience and a network of related connections we build over time. A very large part of the imagery which forms the basis of our metaphorical vocabulary comes from nature. These nature related symbols permeate our language and our collective imaginations.

If a poet uses the image of a garden, we relate to that image by aligning what we already 'know' as 'garden' through our earlier perceptions. This is how we build our response to the poet's 'garden' – we use our total network of internal 'garden' associations to incorporate and assess the poet's image. That is when we have the feeling that we 'know what the poet means.' We recognise and adopt the image as our own.

The metaphor is a bridge between us. It is an integral part of our art and a foundation of a developing culture. We count on our children being able to grasp, invigorate and extend the insight and understanding of the human condition that has come through our cultural evolution in all its breadth.

But to make a metaphor is not simply to take one thing and see it as another, although we can clearly make that work – often as a form of comedy.

'Do you see this bottle? It is like my life!' We *can* make these connections.

If we expect children to study the great poets, playwrights and authors and to do more than reproduce for exam, we need them to be able to recognise themselves and their own experience in the imaginative worlds created.

Children who have an on-going involvement in outdoor learning and are taught in a way that emphasises an experience of nature's subtle connectedness, will have an opportunity at the right age to form their own basis for this cultural understanding. As Richard Louv points out, *'The root of all spiritual life is that early sense of wonder.'* He is speaking about the wonder we feel when faced with the beauty, the power, the delicacy and the majesty of nature. We express those feelings so often in images, and the use of them draws us closer to those feelings once again. Having a sense of polarities, night and day, dark and light, of the part and the whole, of life, growth, death and the patterns and rhythms of the journey between – this sense is born and expanded time and again through our experience of nature and of ourselves in nature and then reinforced and celebrated by our cultural expression.

This is what we base so much of our search for meaning on as we grow into adulthood. We are able to see our own lives in terms of what we come to understand is nature, feeling ourselves a part of it and balancing our own joys and tragedies against what we know as 'life,' as 'natural.' We connect to this nature through experience and we relive and take it into our identity through image and metaphor.

Who's Watching?

One of the most important observations to have come out of the research dedicated to environmental education, is that there are very often intimate links between someone's work or interest in the fields of natural and environmental science and their earlier childhood experiences. Louise Chawla (1998) in her seminal work on significant life experiences looked at the formative influences that appeared to lead to pro-environmental attitudes. She noticed that childhood experiences of natural areas were often cited as a key factor in the respondents' recollections. Those most commonly mentioned in seven surveys of environmental educators or activists were:

Positive experiences in natural areas

Adult role models

Environmental organizations

Education

Negative experiences of environmental degradation

Books and other media

On-the-job experience

Although the recollection-based research has given rise to some academic controversy, it has never-the-less sparked a great deal of on-going interest in the role of nature in childhood but also in the role of the mentor, teacher, adult companion in the process of identification that leads a child to see her/himself as being 'into nature.'

This is a particularly poignant reminder of the position that teachers have in children's lives. They have enormous influence as role models and when we look a little more closely at the types of influence children of different ages experience, it becomes even more poignant. The younger the child, the more the modelling is direct and unconscious. Babies and toddlers learn critical, foundational behaviours such as walking and talking by a complex interplay of inherent cognitive capacities, imitation, creativity and reinforcement. The ability to learn in this way remains with us, evolving along with our levels of experience, habit and thinking.

Albert Bandura's social learning theory, a significant part of the varied and vibrant field of sociological and learning research, has established a basis in science for what we know as common-sense – children learn from the adults around them. The more intimate the relationship between child and adult, the more often, regular and engaged that contact, the deeper the imitation or modelling and therefore the deeper the influence.

Many behaviours, including moral behaviour, attitudes and values can be impacted by imitation and modelling. Because of the nature of outdoor experiences, teachers who are identified by children in that context are likely to be particularly influential. We know that for many reasons, the outdoor experience is memorable for children. We also know that their attention is often far better focused when they are not in the classroom and especially when they are in interesting, challenging environments. And we know that their levels of enjoyment and motivation are high when outdoors. These are three of the four necessary conditions social learning researchers have established as conducive to successful behaviour modelling.

Give children opportunities to explore and practise their own versions of the outdoor experience - setting up and running small, self-managed projects in school, being part of after school clubs with an environmental theme, following up extension work at home, being supported and accompanied by parents, siblings or other carers in similar out-of-school activities – and the fourth condition is met - being able to rehearse and replicate the behaviour independently.

Although teachers may feel that they are teaching content in these situations, in fact there is far more being learned by their pupils. From the way in which we speak about others through to the our enthusiasm and sense of commitment, children take in the whole of the person. Where they identify with the adult, the influence will be deep and life affecting.

The most important attribute we can share with children we teach is our continuing interest in life for all its forms. When we take the focus away from the experience, away from the involvement, we begin to distance ourselves and the child from nature itself. Trying to convey environmental protection concerns for example, clouds the directness of the relationship between child and nature by interceding itself between the two. Our view dominates and colours the independent bond that is forming.

We have to be particularly careful when so much of the motivation for people's interest in nature is based on their fearful concerns for the future of the planet's environmental heritage. There are subtle and fragile aspects of a child's experience of nature, which only become visible in their play and exploration and which we can ignore and even suppress.

'Even if they don't know my 'ditch,' most people I speak with seem to have a ditch somewhere – or a creek, meadow, wood-lot or marsh – that they hold in similar regard. These are places of initiation, where the borders between ourselves and other creatures, where the earth gets under our nails and a sense of place gets under our skin…only the ditches – and the fields, the woods, the ravines – can teach us to care enough for the land.' Pyle (1993)

As an adult, Robert Michael Pyle, a distinguished author and honoured conservationist, studied butterflies and moths. His direct and intimate childhood experiences of nature led him to his environmental work as an adult. Schools can promote this type of relationship for children by encouraging creative and multi-faceted interactions but the teachers themselves are the ones who have the greatest influence. Their values and attitudes, as well as their actual teaching moderates children's connections to nature, the feeling they have, that this is *their place*.

Getting Your Hands Dirty

Several fundamental themes have been introduced which affect the actual teaching and learning practice but also the decisions we make about this practice and the plans we design for its development.

Each of these themes impacts the whole of the teaching and learning, not just what takes place outdoors.

A genuine outdoor learning culture is created from *within* each school as an outcome of practice based on these understandings.

A school needs to develop a whole school outdoor learning culture.

The culture needs to be alive.

Children learn through experience.

The basis for how a child experiences the world is through play.

Play evolves and maturing strands of play behaviour are evident throughout and beyond childhood.

These later behaviours depend on formative, earlier experiences in order to mature developmentally.

The relationship a child has to nature is particularly important for their well-being.

Outdoor learning seeks to encourage children's development by providing for and guiding their experience of nature in an educational setting.

The opportunities offered by outdoor learning in school benefit not only the children but also the teachers and the wider community.

Understanding how to manage best practice outdoor learning in creative and constructive ways encourages teachers' professional development.

Leaders and staff who are able to demonstrate initiative, motivation and a sense of independent responsibility form the essential backbone of a creative and vibrant outdoor learning whole-school culture.

Outdoor Learning is *Not* a Subject

This book is about school. It is about teaching and learning in school, specifically in primary and early years' settings. Although there are wide cross-overs between children's out-of-school and in-school activities, school itself is different. It is about education and has a specific responsibility for the progression of learning. Outdoor learning has as many faces as there are schools looking to explore it and so there is growing pressure to explain what teachers are doing and to demonstrate that what they are doing is appropriate for school and educationally beneficial.

The outdoor learning field is largely undefined, despite having a long history in outdoor education and nature study. There are many people who believe that as a new drive, it offers huge possibilities for improving children's lives, reconnecting to nature, creating a more ecology conscious generation in the face of the climate change and bio-diversity challenges to come, along with tackling the personal and social demands of changing work and home lives in the 21st century.

Understandably, much is promised by passionate supporters. Organisations in the field have grasped the opportunities to promote their work by supporting research, offering funding and creating training programmes, some of which are now providing accredited qualifications. Because this wide-ranging activity is part of a new and open-ended area of education, there is a genuine need to refocus on what a school can provide and how it can do that in the best possible way for all concerned.

One of the main ideas underpinning what I am describing as the whole-school approach is that outdoor learning should not be treated as a subject in itself. It is far better understood and used as a teaching and learning *method*. Moreover, it is a method which is best delivered *by the teachers in the school* as an integrated part of the children's normal work. This is how the children will benefit the most. It is also how the teachers and the rest of the school community will benefit most.

In its most basic form, it means being outside the classroom. I have visited many primary school classes which simply have open doors to a working space adjacent to the classroom itself. Children who choose to, can work in the open air on the same task the class is continuing with indoors.

Teachers report a series of benefits for individuals and interestingly, often for their class-mates too. Some children appear to find it easier to get on with their work while outside, even book work, writing, maths and so on. They may well be those who need quite a lot of attention when in the classroom, unable to concentrate for long periods or remain still for extended lengths of time. In these cases, others in the class certainly benefit too by being able to work in a more settled atmosphere. Teachers also recognise that their own class management is easier and less pressured.

There are however, a great many more advantages for a teaching method which offers the best of outdoor learning than simply being outside. Because it is based on the experiential learning model and applied to an outdoor school situation, children gain from the opportunity of learning through a guided enquiry approach and teachers profit by being able to work with them more creatively.

The inspiration and sense of fulfilment the teachers feel from working with this vibrant approach adds enormous value to their work and to the whole school experience for everyone involved.

Verticality, Horizontality, Embedding

Whole-school outdoor learning depends on there being both vertical and horizontal linking throughout the school's curriculum. Continuity in both directions means that the children will have many opportunities to become familiar with content and to develop skills. But it also means that they will be able to re-visit and re-experience similar activities, often in the same or similar environments, both in and out of school. Revisiting, in new and progressive ways allows children to deepen their knowledge and appreciation. Very importantly, it focuses the experience, not simply on collecting information but also on a broader learning range, as well as the nature of the environment itself.

Some schools, for example have created a small farm yard or part of a farm yard within the school grounds and incorporated it as part of the children's routines. Raising chickens, collecting eggs and caring for a small flock of hens can be a wonderfully enriching activity in a child's life. The understanding, levels of care and responsibility are clearly different for early years children compared to those in the upper primary. Older children may, for example be able to monitor and record the chickens' growth as an on-going IT study, discovering and maintaining the most suitable environment for the flock's health. There is genuine potential for on-going and increasing benefit, building on earlier experiences if children are able to participate meaningfully in such an activity on a regular basis.

Play/Work

I was always intrigued by the 'craze' whenever it appeared in my schools. All of a sudden, it seemed, everyone was doing 'it.' I remember bizarre examples from my own childhood – a boys' school, the sixth and seventh years sitting on the playground 'monkey bars' and climbing frames, blowing soapy bubbles across the school yard. Was it because the 'tools of the trade' had just then become available in the shops?

When I was teaching I certainly noticed that the children often 'came across' something that immediately inspired mass involvement. Think of the rain storm and the immediate fun in the puddles which follows.

A small field belonging to the school where I was teaching eight year olds had the hay cut. It had hardly sat for long enough to begin to dry before the children had discovered it. Soon it was the whole school's focus during break times. Houses, castles, villages, an entire township, it seemed, sprang up in a matter of minutes and began to grow in an ever more complex series of dwellings, paths and roads. Children organised themselves into teams of carriers, builders, negotiators and then, of course soldiers, defenders of the territory.

Beyond the spontaneous however, it became clear to me that certain play crazes occurred regularly within generalised age groups. I had a far better than even chance to stimulate something very similar if they didn't seem to be happening from the children's own volition. I simply had to leave something about that 'matched' the expected behaviour.

One of the most exciting and on-going stimuli to this kind of activity that the children 'discovered' was ten tons of soil! In no time at all it became a swarm of children, digging, sculpting, building. Homes were dug. Mines and quarries appeared. Fairy houses tucked themselves into safe corners of the mound.

I began to form a rough, working schema from the activities I had observed which exhibited that all-encompassing 'craze' element. Interestingly, it seemed to follow a loosely evolutionary pattern: nomadic hunters and gatherers, atavism, settlements, farming, tools, separation, social management, collecting and organising, science, development of social resources i.e. natural engineering, explorers, journeys, bringing home treasure, exporting culture. Although all children love animals, if I brought a couple of lambs that needed feeding and looking after into a class of nine and ten year olds, there was likely to be a very different response in terms of on-going, independent commitment and care.

I discovered David Sobel's work (2008) recently and he has come across a similar pattern, which he calls 'play motifs.'

Regardless of socioeconomic status, ethnicity or ecosystem, children play in similar ways when they have safe, free time in nature...Spend time in a safe, woodsy playground and you'll find children:

(1)   making forts (dens) and special places

(2)   playing hunting and gathering games

(3)   shaping small worlds

(4)   developing friendships with animals

(5)   constructing adventures

(6)   descending into fantasies

(7)   following paths and figuring out short-cuts

He sees these motifs played out throughout childhood and as such they *'function at right angles'* to age and maturation groupings. You will remember my discovery of the bike track in the copse – a 'special place' for older children and a clear example of the den or fort-building motif.

What children learn when they are able to engage in their play at these levels provides the healthy scaffolding for their 'work.' When they are young, their play *is* their work and to some extent these two modes of interaction separate out as they get older. Many will describe them however, as different activities altogether. Never-the-less, children of primary school age bridge these two worlds, one flowing into and informing the other.

Concentration and prolonged focus, attentiveness, patience, resilience, orderliness, imaginative grasp, mental picturing and the ability to visualise and manipulate imagery, memory, fine and gross motor coordination, sensitivity of perception, ability to use all the senses, balance and centeredness – the list runs on and on – the development of which is rooted in constructive, experiential play leading to essential aspects of our ability to work.

We see this ability unfold in a child's life when we incorporate its development vertically and horizontally through the curriculum and the actual processes of teaching and learning. Outdoor, experiential learning allows us to match the content of activities closely to the natural motifs of children's play, drawing out the more formal aspects of 'work' from the informal nature of 'play.'

Verticality through the years encourages progression. Horizontal linking within the same year's curriculum, on the other hand, while clearly supporting progression because one topic follows another, has the added value of placing the focus more on developing key outdoor learning skills. Unless activities continue through the seasons, such as caring for gardens and animals, teachers are unlikely to use the same tasks again within their topics too closely to one another. The particular skills being learned are, however likely to be the same. Seeing them through the eyes of different activities and topics reinforces the nuances of their development. They span the boundaries between activities to create a developing thread over the course of the school year.

When the outdoor learning practice is an integral part of the formal learning in the school, planned for and managed vertically and through each year horizontally, we describe it as being embedded.

Embedding outdoor learning is a challenge to achieve, both for school leaders and the teachers themselves. It is however, the basis for building a whole-school culture and is a necessary goal to set and to achieve if the outdoor learning is to actually make the differences and realise the gains that are claimed for it.

Diversions & Dead-Ends

It is easy for a school to become diverted in its focus. With plenty of funding and a lot of early enthusiasm around for school outdoor learning development for a few years, head teachers saw many opportunities but little clear direction. Raised 'edible garden' beds and outdoor 'classrooms' began to spring up everywhere. Creating new and exciting projects has always been one of the ways heads can inspire interest and engagement in the school's development. These tangible 'proofs of progress' helped to maintain parental and community involvement, but the new 'classroom' seldom increased on-going outdoor activity and the garden beds tended to be relegated to after-school club, unusable as a class resource.

Without being fully embedded and without a genuine whole-school culture to support it, the outdoor learning is piecemeal and disjointed. Schools with this approach rely on enthusiastic individuals to carry the role of advocate for taking children outdoors. Normally s/he is given the title of outdoor coordinator, without real powers but expected to be responsible for inspiring others, recommending resources, offering suggestions for lessons and organising whatever outdoor tools and resources the school has. S/he becomes the 'go to' person for everything 'outdoor learning.' If we are looking for a more sustainable way of evolving our curriculum, it cannot rely for its development on the enthusiasm of one or two advocates.

Outdoor projects introduced in an 'added-on' style, may only serve to complicate and compact timetables which are already under stress. It is important that there is a calm and predictable work life in the school. Modern life styles are hectic enough already. This means that where a new set of ideas and projects is introduced, the outdoor learning needs to be planned for and embedded so that it does not end up adding to the confusion.

The 'graveyard' is a normal outcome of this system. But there are other problems related to it, taking the school's focus away from building a more sustainable system which can deliver the goals set for it.

Buying in expertise, for example can certainly be problematic, tending to be something of a double-edged sword approach. Interestingly, the first of the key recommendations of the Natural England Report - 092 (2012) is that 'the role of providers in providing coherent CPD must not be neglected.' This is based on the view of Tabbush and O'Brien (2003) that *'schools and teachers cannot be expected to take total responsibility for environmental and outdoor education.'* Given that there may well be a concern, even by teachers themselves over whether they have the confidence and competence to deliver a robust outdoor learning programme, it is understandable that professional development training is seen as an important element in the process of successful delivery. There are however, essential differences in the way trainings are planned and providers see their role and the last thing schools need is to be swayed by opportunistic service providers.

Often what happens is that there is a flurry of inspired activity after 'expert' input, which is then followed by a general return to normal patterns as soon as the typical pressures of school life set in. Teachers may well be persuaded of the benefits of outdoor learning but the fact that it requires an actual change in habits and a change in the day to day teaching methods is usually a step too far for most. In order to build teaching expertise, the professional development of individual staff members needs to take place in a wider culture of shared staff development.

Teachers need to be able to plan together and practise together. The responsibility and the experience need to be a shared, whole-school endeavour. Reviewing, remodelling and moving forward are all key aspects which work best as an openly rehearsed, collective school exercise.

'Expertise' is normally impressive of course, especially for teachers who feel overworked and under prepared. Outdoor activities appear inspiring for their simplicity and immediacy. Those who are already enthusiastic and wanting to get on with their first 'project' are easily captivated. But it is a common experience in schools that once the expert has gone, so has the 'event.' Teachers are left with very little to go on. They have not had any genuine development of their own ability to connect outdoor activities directly to content.

Although they may have been convinced by the inspiring demonstration of what is possible, what they do not need is another set of activities they might or might not choose to do. They need a way to change the deeper structures of their own teaching practice. When I first began teaching I was taken 'under the wing' by an older colleague who had many years of teaching experience behind him and who was widely known for being both inspiring and authoritative. The children loved to be in his class and the other teachers relied on him endlessly.

'The first time you are in front of a class,' he told me, *'and every time you feel really pressured as a teacher after that, your initial tendency is to teach exactly as you have*

been taught yourself. You go back to what feels safe, whether it's the kind of teacher you want to be or not. It takes hard work and a strong desire to be anything different.'

We all revert to what we know and if people lack confidence in their own abilities, then even more so. Investment in professional development needs this focus, so teachers actually take on change and can move forward enthusiastically with new methods that work and demonstrate progression.

Forest school, for example, has become one of the most recognised promoters of expertise in this area and they offer a recognised qualification for their training. There was funding support for some time for teachers to train as forest school practitioners themselves, even for schools to employ independent part time practitioners to take classes outdoors regularly.

Of course, with the pace of school, the number of activities constantly taking place and the work load for teachers, it is only a matter of time before the status quo returns, if a school does employ somebody part-time. Class teachers are drawn away to meetings, preparation and other demands and the forest school activity tends to become isolated.

For many the idea of forest school has come to mean the same as outdoor learning. Unfortunately this is far from true and has tended to slow the process of embedding school-based outdoor learning and creating a whole-school culture in favour of having a time-tabled forest school session once a week. In effect it has distracted schools from developing their own teacher-based expertise and allowed the 'buy-in' method to give the appearance of the school being much more than it actually is as an 'outdoor learning school.'

The Nuts & Bolts

Before we look at what to do and how to do it, we need to emphasise again that we are looking for genuine school work. The subject work needs to be served by the outdoor learning, not the other way round. Its role is to stimulate and strengthen the other work as an exciting, engaging way to experience and understand those subjects. The central focus must be on teaching and learning and not be deflected into areas that appear, at least in the short term to be easier to provide for than dealing with this core issue.

You will need to ask some straightforward questions to find out where the outdoor learning is up to in your school at the moment. As there are probably already several years' legacy of on-off projects and schemes, the time to get the programme and the processes in order is absolutely as soon as possible to really make a difference. The longer the outdoor learning goes on without being fully embedded, the greater the chance that it will fade away as a nice but undeveloped idea.

Step 1: Connections

You'll need to find out exactly what is taking place – how, when, where and why - and you will also need to map it out so that the particular areas which are not strong can be highlighted. This overview is really important because you can then see the connections between the different activities over time and across the year groups. These connections point to critical areas to do with embedding, progression and integration.

Remember the 'graveyard?' Each of those 'monuments' has a history. Are there links between them? Does one follow another? Have different classes explored similar tasks? Or are they isolated testimonials, pointing to individual teacher initiative rather than whole school planning?

Step 2: Evidence

During this initial period it is ideal to be collecting and collating any evidence you have, in order to show what outdoor learning has been taking place. This includes all the portfolio evidence schools are accustomed to assembling, such as teacher planning, examples of children's work, assessments, and reviews along with photo and video recordings. You may well find that there is a lot more going on than you expected, but not necessarily with a clear or shared direction.

Step 3: When & Where?

Having gathered the evidence base together, it needs to be used to provide an overview for what has happened/is happening and when it took/takes place. This is really like the skeleton. It doesn't let us know anything in detail about depth of experience, but it does make it very clear what the overall picture is.

Set out a school year table divided into weeks and year groups. Highlight the terms and include the relevant school calendar features such as sports' days, book days, festival celebrations and so on. Enter all the outdoor learning activity that has actually taken place up to the present into the table and then include the planned-for activities to the end of the year.

This will immediately highlight patterns over time - which year groups have more outdoor learning, whether the learning is regular and often and where there are obvious gaps and differences you might not have expected. Seeing the pattern is what gives you a clear overview, which then allows you to dig deeper into the detail.

Step 4: Processes

Once you have a structural map of how the outdoor learning is taking place in the school, you need to have a closer look at the processes involved in the key activities. In the foundation stage, for example, we have already noted that there is likely to be a great deal more outdoor learning going on than the rest of the school. We know that the higher up the year groups we go, the less outdoor work takes place. The pressures of subject content and testing determine the way it is taught. At least, the teachers' perceptions of those constraints determine how it is taught. Early years' experiences are often very open-ended activities such as everyday walks. When the children are older they tend to be more involved in 'one-off,' end-of-term and pre-summer holiday outdoor projects.

Never-the-less, we need to have a clear idea of the processes no matter what the style of the activity. They involve the preparation and follow up work as much as what happens during the actual task itself. Any deep-level integration of outdoor learning into the rest of the children's work depends on these preliminary and closing processes, directing the children's engagement and providing an interpretive experience to develop meaning beyond the immediate event.

At this early stage in building a comprehensive school overview of what takes place and how it takes place in the outdoor learning, it is very important not to be overly critical of what is or is not discovered. The most useful outcome is simply to have a thorough description. This will form the basis for how to go forward. It will show clearly where good practice is taking place, who has both the experience and the confidence to take the process forward and who will need more supportive input.

Step 5: Policy

This next step, comparing what you find in the audit with what you would like the school to be achieving, is a familiar but essential procedure all the same, to progress in an organised and guided way. But you will need some form of policy document to outline what your outdoor learning goals are for the school, covering at least the areas I have outlined below. The document establishes your intention and because it is public, makes clear to parents and the wider community, not only what you want to achieve, but also what you have put in place to ensure it does in truth come about.

There is an example document for you to use as a guide in the appendices. It must be real however, everything firmly based on your own school and the community you actually serve. Think through your own processes and change as necessary what I have set out. No doubt there will be areas you decide not to use and others which you will add. Treat it as a working document.

Rationale & aims

Teaching & learning expectations

Planning & assessment

Professional development

Health & Safety

Parents & community

Grounds development

Provision of resources

Step 6: How & Why?

With the annual table as a starting point, you are then able to speak to teachers directly about what they have been doing so you can build a much deeper picture of the involvement children have in the outdoor learning. You can talk through and mark up regular and repeated activities as well as seeing how those particular experiences have been developed as a wider part of their work, comparing it with the portfolio evidence you have already assembled. You will begin to see the processes teachers have used for these activities and how thought-through the preparation and follow up is.

Gaining this level of insight is critical because you can then gauge not only the quality of the way activities are presented but also the horizontal connections over the year, giving you a sense of how the progression of particular skills is managed.

Separate if you can, the evidence for what has been taught from what has been learned. Wherever possible, use the children's experiences to give an idea of their level of learning. Compiling their written and artistic responses is hugely helpful early in the process. It will set the tone and give guidance for later evaluation and assessment work.

Make sure you look at children with specific support needs and identify where more time outside might be beneficial. Look at whether outdoor learning objectives have been incorporated into individual education plans.

It is also important to look closely at how parents, carers and the wider community have been involved. Whole-school outdoor learning is not something schools should try to develop without parent input, at the very least when considering how to resolve the dreaded wet-weather clothing issues. In fact, as I have argued, there are huge positives for opening the whole thing out, making it a truly community-based endeavour and measuring parent involvement needs a similar overview – who has been involved, when and doing what. If we want to engage parents and carers, along with community expertise we have to take a proactive stance, searching out and connecting with the ones who do not already appear to take an active part in their children's school lives. This is one of the areas which has been very successful for schools managing positive, outreaching programmes.

It's Never What to Teach; It's *How* to Teach

Great outdoor teaching is not really any different to great classroom teaching but teachers do often feel that going outdoors with classes can be challenging. Looking for ideas about *what* to teach takes the focus away from what really has to adapt in a teacher's work. If we want our schools to create genuine outdoor learning cultures we have to look at *how* we teach.

The most important ingredient in working successfully with children is the teacher's *sense of confidence*. This is the same indoors as it is outdoors. But the confidence needs to be based on secure preparation, having the trust of the children and being able to manage their behaviour. In an outdoor environment it can be demanding. It has to be real, not based on being bigger, stronger and louder. Ultimately, that sense of discipline is what gives the children a feeling of security and a mood of calm direction – essential for good teaching and learning.

Whose Discipline?

The *preliminary and closing processes* along with the idea of *interpretive experience* are the key structural elements that span the whole of an outdoor learning activity. It is not so much a teaching style as it is a *method* for engaging children. In order to begin building progressive school-based outdoor experiences however, the children need to be in the right state of mind.

One of the greatest challenges for many teachers taking children out of the classroom is dealing with class behaviour. Quality outdoor learning begins with the children being 'in hand,' so sooner or later the question of discipline always arises. Can teachers oversee and direct their classes in such a way that the children remain focused, enthusiastic and engaged at the appropriate level throughout the task?

I often work with schools to demonstrate and lead what can be done - creating an outdoor learning festival for the whole school, for example. Having set up a 'camp' at the edge of the grounds, I'll wait for the classes to come over for their activity. It is always particularly interesting to see the way classes approach, and of course, it is all down to the teacher.

This happens all the time. I see the 'herd' stampeding from the classroom in the distance. Usually one or two boys are leading the pack, racing at full tilt, arms flailing, shouting out, *'There's a fire. Look, there's a fire!'* The rest of the children are stretched out in a long line, back towards the 'good girls,' hanging on to the skirts of the teaching assistant. The entire charge is accompanied by the punctuated shouts of their class teacher to stop and come back, having been held up in the classroom trying to find James' lost wellie boot and Annie's gloves!

If I walk towards them just a little, standing away from the canopy, arms out as the children run towards me, I can 'catch' the front-runners before they race into my camp, without having to say anything, simply by my presence. The rest of the class is drawn to this point and gradually they all gather together expectantly. If I don't answer questions or get drawn into any conversation, I can establish a relaxed, safe and attentive mood. By then the teacher will have arrived, apologising profusely while the teaching assistant continues the hubbub at the back of the group in raised whispers, attempting to deal with several requests at once.

Management is everything. If we want the children to benefit from being outdoors, we have to prepare them *to be able* to benefit. This means their teachers must understand what it means to have their classes in a 'ready' state and be able to practise it successfully.

As I go from school to school I come across the same thing – So many teachers love the idea of outdoor learning, love the whole thing - except the bit about actually going outside. I used to think it was because of what they rather shame-facedly confided. It's uncomfortable outdoors; the weather's cold, rainy, too hot, too cold, too windy, not windy enough!

But I have my doubts about such admissions. I actually think it is to do with feeling insecure in a variety of ways

64

and the greatest of these is the feeling that Johnny and Adam and even Susan are going to tear away into the distance and throw themselves from the nearest cliff onto the road below, where a bus full of inspectors will run them over and finally finish them off - with poor Ms White, the teacher, torn between shouting for help from the top of the cliff and helping Marlene and her best friend, Walter finally squeeze into their outdoor clothing all the way back at the classroom!

Being outdoors with children is actually simple and, easy, so long as the teacher is in the right frame of mind. And the way to do that is to give very clear messages that you *really are* in control – of yourself as well as of the situation. The children need to know that you can be relied upon at all times - but it doesn't work by telling them that! Shrieking at the top of your voice, as they disappear over the crest in front of you, that you are in charge and they'd better come back - only tells them that you are not in control at all. The 'messages' need to be practical, convincing and straight forward.

On the other hand, there are the fun-lovers, the teachers who like to run about and jump up and down with the children. They do have a certain level of success even if they do tend to be the ones shouting, '*Come on. Look. There's a fire,*' at the charge. Unfortunately, you can't get away from the fact that you are the adult – great fun or not. In the eyes of the children you are expected to be the one responsible, the leader, not the led. Underneath everything else, they depend on you.

Why does this matter? Because some children, not necessarily all children, will take on the sense of responsibility for others and for themselves if you do not. They are aware that there is a vacuum of responsibility. Even if they don't act or show it outwardly, they feel anxious for others in the group. At the same they are divided in their feelings towards the teacher; on the one hand wanting to feel respect for and secure in your presence while at the same time disappointed and vulnerable because they perceive that there is a lack of security. All this can happen unconsciously of course, but it affects them all the same. We teach the children far more than the content of our lessons. We teach them who we are.

Confidence & Engagement

This is my personal list of headings for the 'how' essentials, I use when training to build *teachers' confidence* and *children's engagement.*

Be the first

Games

Boundaries

Habits

Voice

A sense of presence

Being the author

Simple & achievable

Practise the process

Imagery

Groupings

Clear intentions

When you leave the classroom to go outside with the children, **be the first** out of the door. Be the first into the outdoor learning classroom, into the forest clearing. Make it your space into which you welcome them. It means having the children in the right frame of mind before you leave, ready to follow, having made sure that all of the children have been taken care of before you leave.

Have things ready. Be prepared, really prepared. Absolutely make sure, especially the first time you ever do something new, that you know the site yourself, have visited it and spent time in it recently as part of your preparations. The last thing you need and certainly the children need, is for you to be scrabbling about looking for items of kit or wondering what exactly the next step was in the process.

This does the same thing as being there first. It shows whose space it is. It's a territorial statement and one which the children will unconsciously respect. They feel safe and special being welcomed into it. It heightens their senses and makes the experience that much more memorable.

Think of a group of children outside as being like a dandelion clock - seeds blowing in the wind. If you want to gather them, you have to catch them as they come to rest, so you need to create particular resting moments when you can actually catch their attention. This is why people have them run away and then back again, in a hundred variations. It creates a rhythm of expansion - away and then contraction – back. At the point of contraction you have one of those resting moments. They run up to you with eager anticipation. There's your chance. Show them how to sit, where to sit. Bring a moment of culture into the nature.

It places you in the centre, as the leader, as the 'first.' This is all about a natural sense of authority bringing security and confidence to the children.

Use game mentality to capture their interest. What's a game? Routine, rhythm, rules, boundaries and a journey. Every game is a journey - a metaphor for something deep in our make-up as human beings. Every journey is leading somewhere and children love a game for the inner resonance and reassurance of it. A game is a story unfolding, carrying us somewhere. It leads the children to moments of punctuation in the rush of activity where you can 'catch' them again.

Being able to work with the rhythm and movement of the class develops deep trust in the teacher by the children. It helps to eliminate the squabbling, bickering and petty competitions of the group. It allows the group to flow and leads them back into being able to engage – to play to explore, to discover and to work.

Gather together at the beginning of the activity.

Start together. Don't begin until everyone is ready and with you.

Always think of an activity, in or outdoors as a 'social' activity.

Refer to 'we' and make the social aim clear. *'We're just about there. We've got everyone on board now. Are we on target for what we want to get done?'*

Practise first. This lets you adjust, affirm and progress, before you actually get started 'for real.' It allows children to be successful.

Have safety zones – time and place. A corner in the class room for a moment's quiet 'time out,' an opportunity to choose a less challenging version, an accepted time for a pause or a chat.

Know how the activity ends. Make sure everybody knows.

Know what a really successful session would be like. Give it a name. 'First rate, top of the order, my number one,' Refer to it and aim for it as a group. Make sure everybody knows. Reward progress toward it.

By introducing actual games, you can establish a set of boundaries in an easy-to-grasp-remember-and-practise form for the children. There may be physical outer limits for the game. 'Not past the trees over there. No further than the path.' You can create these limits for behaviour as well, for starting or finishing an activity, gathering together for example. 'All hands on deck!' meaning everyone has to be touching a tree, the fence, standing on the path, sitting in a circle or on a log in front of you – whatever you have in your environment.

You can introduce commands. 'All in,' called out in a sing-song game playing voice. Once learned, the architecture of the game can be used for your outdoor activities, giving the teacher an enormous reach and children an easily recognisable form to follow.

This idea of architecture or structure is very helpful not only for activities, but also for the general run of the day, particularly for change moments - starting, stopping. Any part of the process that is repeated until it **forms a habit** takes a lot of weight off everybody.

Habits, in this context, are like game elements which are internalised, encouraging the smooth flow of class dynamics. If we treat these processes like a repertoire, like a script, repeating the same elements in the same order, we encourage less stressful movement and interaction based on predictable structures.

Like a repertoire however, it needs to be kept fresh. The habits have a 'shelf-life' and will stop working after a time.

Our skill as a teacher is to recognise this change before it happens and already introduce enough modification to satisfy the need for change while maintaining the steadiness everyone relies upon. Children get 'lost' in hectic environments. These same principles apply outdoors in how we manage our classes as much as when we are indoors - and particularly at the change-over from one environment to the other.

Do it before you need to. Practise the return. Reward them for their good work. Send them off again. It is a musical thing. It has to do with structure and with rhythm. You get a sense for it. You get to trust it. And the children learn it and trust it like a song, like a well-loved game.

Listen to the sound of their work *and* their play. This cannot be emphasised enough. The tones and the volumes will tell you when it is time to draw them in again. You will be able to notice this before you will actually *see* anything. This is what the older teachers call, 'Having eyes in the back of your head.'

Once you start to pay attention to the sound, you notice things that you were unaware of before. You can hear constructive activity. You can hear a change coming as the volume begins to increase and the pitch rises. If you want the children to develop their senses then you have to start with yourself.

Just as the tones and volume of the children's interactions tell you a great deal about the quality of their work and play, so the **tone and volume of our own voices** is also critical. Every school seems to have at least one teacher who can 'stop a child at thirty paces' with her voice. It's very common. unless the head teacher has had an inspired recruitment policy in place for some time.

Often the owner of the heart-arresting 'teacher's voice' is also not one to waste energy moving unnecessarily about. Think of concentric circles, like ripples, spreading out from the teacher in the centre. The first circle stops at arm's reach. The next is a step away. After that it's various measures of the increasing power of the voice. This teacher is far less likely to walk over to a child in order to have a quiet word, pick up the ball or guide an action in a positive direction. For them it's the sword. First option. Look up from the teacher's desk. *'James! Put that down!'*

Job done.

The mood of any class is governed by a teacher's ability to maintain the rhythm of the learning in time with progressive, engaging and challenging activities. Although it's often the 'thirty paces teacher' who stands at the top of the school's discipline tree, practising true leadership, so that the children *willingly* follow, requires something different of a teacher. **It requires a teacher's natural sense of presence**.

Gather the children close. Do not give instructions until everybody is 'with you.' Do not allow little Suzie or Archie to continue an on-going conversation with the teaching assistant. Stop the assistant from doing it. Do not allow the teaching assistant to herd children to you or instruct the children to listen. Do not have children telling others to stop talking. They are not the teacher. The assistant is not the teacher. You are the teacher.

To go a little more deeply, the 'teacher' is a role, something you share with the other teachers in the eyes of the children, a part of the relationship structure. You are playing a part and it takes genuine heart and skill to play the part with integrity. But it is not entirely you the children look up to - not you in an egotistical sense. It is you, playing the role of their teacher, of the guiding leader. If you bond too closely, egotistically to the role, feeling the power of it over the children, you become frightening. You may well have control. But you will no longer have their trust.

This is a very difficult, but absolutely critical balance to find and teachers struggle with it in so many ways. When you have a number of adults working together to lead a class, you need to play the role very clearly and the other adults need to play their parts equally clearly. I see the problems that arise and are then compounded over and over working with teachers and classes outdoors. No one should collude with any behaviour that undermines a straight forward, relaxed and secure relationship between the class and their teacher, especially not the teacher.

Authority is also enhanced by actually being **the 'author' of ideas and projects**, leading the creative drive in the class by example. Being a creative teacher is essential for great teaching. Feeling that your own 'creativity' is not good enough is no help to the children. It communicates the wrong message unfortunately. From time to time your own efforts are by far the most important for them. It is not a question of quality. It is a question of identity. They need to be led by example. Being a pointer won't do it for them. You have to be a creator. The action is what inspires children, not the outcome.

Because going outdoors is different, you need to give the children a chance to learn *how* to be outdoors. You need to **practise the process first**. They may well be so excited that they can't concentrate sufficiently to get down to the task you have in mind. You need to train them to be able to get to the working state in stages.

Putting all their kit on and making it outside to come to you as a quiet, in-hand group, ready for the next step may well be all you can manage to start with. It is far better to reward them immediately with that success by letting them explore freely than persevering with anything else and introducing the chance of 'messing up.'

Work with them in stages, a little at a time. Keep the goals uncomplicated and attainable. Being able to go out in a concentrated but relaxed state, carry out a straightforward, quick task and be back in the classroom in good order is a great step in the right direction. If you are clear, for example that the first 'task' might be as humble as looking at a grass flower for thirty seconds, or lying on your back by yourself to watch the clouds for a minute, in order to write a poem about what you experienced back in the classroom, then it is easy to see how we can build up the 'skills' of observation and recollection in simple steps.

Having already pointed to the power and importance of **natural metaphor** in education and cultural heritage, I shall come back to the use of imagery later, when we look at horizontal development and the use of narrative as a key part in the preliminary process.

The **groupings** we choose make a real difference to the quality of what is achieved outdoors. Children associate being able to play with being outdoors and because most adults think that play equals 'letting off steam,' they are accustomed to doing just that – running around and making a lot of noise. They tend to differentiate school work from free play, where 'free' means to do what they please, which is the likely outcome when you first ask them, in their groups to get on with the task independently. There will be some confusion about how to go about it for some of the children, not necessarily about the task instructions but certainly about the manner of behaviour. Is it work or play?

Not so long ago I had a class of eight year olds in the woods with their teachers for the day. We had spent most of the morning and lunch working through several activities in order for them to get closer to being able to play constructively and independently for some of the time in the afternoon.

It can take several sessions for them to begin to engage more naturally and creatively. An informal group of about ten boys all began to 'work' at a large root of a tree that had collapsed. It offered a place to dig, to hide and to build up a 'camp.' They were fully engaged, lots of shouting, developing a story about what they were doing, dirt going in all directions, several of them hauling in sticks and branches and with plenty of animated discussion about who should do what and how.

It was a primitive start. They had a fantastic time, but in the end the entire site was more or less demolished. They had worn it down to nothing. All that remained was the hard base of the root. The piles of dirt had been shifted and lay spread about on the forest floor. It is no wonder so many adults are very cautious about letting children dive properly into their play.

The next time they were in the woods, they began to build. And this time ended up with a complex series of small rooms made of sticks around the root base. The rooms made up the operating decks of a tank and they had gun barrels and helicopter landing pads, steering gear and most importantly a narrative they all shared. When they left, the tank remained. To anyone else it looked like a pile of sticks and branches. To them it had become something real.

The boundaries between play and work are particularly mobile for younger children like this. As their social interaction develops, it can be helpful to introduce the idea of **formal and informal work modes** to distinguish the type of behaviour needed. Informal work needs free conversation and lots of contained interaction. Formal work, on the other hand requires a very much quieter atmosphere, independent focus and attention entirely on the task.

Choosing groupings according to the informal or formal type of work allows teachers to encourage better work focus. Clearly you will expect constructive outcomes from each style of working, but the actual output may come in different forms - written data collection, organised and thorough, as a result of formal outdoor observation, a series of challenging questions or impressions to use as a collage of inspirations for creative writing from an informal session.

Knowing what it is that you want to achieve with a particular activity is vital. As I have discussed above, it is absolutely fine to have modest aims. It is actually much better to have a simple and manageable goal than to overcomplicate things. The potential personal and social development outcomes outdoor learning offers are certainly the aim of any school looking to deepen its outdoor provision, but **aims for an activity should be straightforward and easily recognised**. The intangibles we need to leave to a more sophisticated analysis than we have at our fingertips.

It is very important not to get the aims mixed up however. If you are wanting an exploratory activity and your goal is that the children should record their discoveries to bring back into the classroom, then the step of recording or documenting – writing, drawing, photographing and so on becomes the aim - not the quality of the recording. But if the quality of the recording is poor, then there needs to be a separate set of activities which places the focus specifically on improving that process.

This is where the 'skills' are built up. Breaking what appear to be very open-ended activities into skills-based learning opportunities means that we introduce progression in the development. The general activity may still seem similarly open-ended - outdoors, digging about under the trees - but having a clear and achievable aim as a focus makes it part of a sequence. And this sequence starts to form the structure of the actual learning in the outdoors.

Resource 'Junkies'

It's a rare school I visit where most teachers, when faced with a new topic to develop and teach, don't make a favourite online resource site their first port-of-call. It seems that instead of being the author and creating content themselves in direct response to their children's needs, they feel more secure with someone else's lesson plans, ideas and methods.

Is it because they think it's a tried and tested activity or lesson scheme? Or is it because they have lost the confidence in, maybe even the ability to develop their own content? They are certainly far more likely to depend on what they think is an outside authority - and the resource sites, advertising their content as 'genuine lessons created by real teachers,' offers this sense of authority.

There are several effects; the worst of them that the children do not have an on-going, integrated outdoor learning path based on their own experiences. One 'resource' idea does not necessarily lead to further progressive development. So the teacher goes back to find a new resource to introduce instead of seeing the child's experience as a springboard for the next step in a developing sequence.

Unfortunately, the trend is definitely toward 'resource site dependence' and it means that teachers are taking entire outdoor learning topics off the internet and plugging them into their term's planning. The focus for the planning is no longer the children, the work itself or the teacher's creative response to those needs. It is dictated by the online resource opportunities.

But it's not only children who lose out. Teachers neglect their own creative development. When this happens, a central key to their own fulfilment through their work is undermined.

The Vertical & Horizontal Axes

Planning for Embedded Verticality

It is very common to see the planning for outdoor learning based entirely on school development plans – Teachers look around the school for 'great outdoor ideas,' and their 'home improvement, landscaping monsters' come out of hiding.

We could develop the front entrance to the school by planting a hedge along the fence. We could build an outdoor classroom by the pond. We could create a story space with benches and a shaded area.

Although this sort of physical product looks impressive when you visit schools it has very little to do with outdoor learning. It is conceived from an adult's perspective. *But we consulted the children. They came up with their ideas and we looked at what was possible,* I keep being told. If it were a genuine consultation based on children's views only, schools would have a complex of large swimming pools with slides, rides and an option to turn it into a ski run in the winter, attached to a cross country bike track with an eventing ring for ponies, depending on the particular loves of the dominant social group in the oldest class.

Children are easily led, want to please and are generally reasonable. When it comes to the discussion part of the consultation, so long as they feel there is some fun and excitement in it for them, they will be happy to accept the outdoor classroom and even the story telling circle. It all comes down to the quality of the pitch.

We need to plan for the children's *learning experience*. Whenever possible plan together. Allocate a shared planning time each term to generate collaboration and peer training in relation to projects, subject specialisms and wider work within the school.

It is easiest to think of the planning as either class or school based as rough working definitions to help separate the areas of focus. Activities that are generated by class work are on the whole, experienced by the particular class whereas school based activities are shared by all or at least many of children.

When you plan around an annual school calendar, you have the perfect vehicle for creating a whole-school outdoor learning structure. These are events which the whole school will take part in and which provide opportunities both for connecting class work with the event and also sharing a whole-school outdoor celebration when appropriate. This is ideal for a sense of verticality in the curriculum.

Generally speaking, younger children will spend more time outdoors on a regular basis than the older years. Calendar-based events are very important for the older children's work, allowing their teachers to incorporate meaningful outdoor learning components into their programmes of study.

Annual religious celebrations, seasonal festivals, art and science weeks are all important opportunities for teachers to use as whole school 'punctuation points' in the term. An essential aspect of embedded verticality in the outdoor learning programme is the predictability for children of returning events. It is far better to maintain a calendar's structure and salient features, once it is established, rather than changing it each year.

Encouraging children's expectations is an essential tool for supporting their engagement. They look forward to important events coming up where they will have a particular part to play, growing responsibilities to carry and their chance to lead. It allows them to learn from the children who have gone before and to place themselves in the history, the sense of time and place as they see how eventually, they too will become the 'older ones.'

These events also allow teachers of older classes to focus their outdoor learning work on that event and then move on to other demands. It provides a stable structure for the rhythm of the timetable rather than having people cramming in order to allocate time. Time pressure, as a result of poor planning always results in learning experiences which are less worthwhile for the class.

Topics & Projects

Many primary schools choose to work with topics or projects in order to deliver their curriculum. They find that if carefully planned, a thematic approach supports children's natural curiosity and creativity. Other schools feel they can encourage a similar way of working and learning by using regular projects throughout the term. In either case, the idea is to offer children an opportunity for direct experience in a meaningful context to encourage higher order thinking.

As it is a relatively new system for primary schools in the UK, teachers are experimenting with topic choices and development. Education companies are already selling pre-designed topics and teacher resource sites are filled with a 'rich' assortment of possibilities.

The choice of topics is hugely influential on the verticality of the outdoor learning programme. If topics are being chosen independently and according to the interests of the teachers or suggested by the discovery of a particular online resource, the curriculum organisation can become loose, even at times, random. This is especially so when teachers are concentrating on skills over content and the topic role is used principally to attract children's interest.

It is a very positive step in the right direction to encourage teachers to be more creative but there is a danger that making up new topic themes each year can weaken a rich opportunity for deepening children's engagement.

Where year group topics are stable, the children will look forward to what is to come. This is very important for the vertical nature of outdoor learning development where the building up and progression of learning over time requires a number of returns to similar, but developing experiences.

The difference is marked between a woodland wellie walk in the foundation stage and a focused study of a tree's annual life-cycle by eleven year olds in the same copse. There is a great deal to be gained from returning to the same place and exploring the same events. Although the experiences and the learning will progressively change, the relationship between them will form a strong foundation for the engagement with nature that best practice outdoor learning is looking to achieve.

Linking Back – Content Threads

There are two ways we can develop verticality in the curriculum using content threads. They are related, but approach the content from slightly different directions. I spend a lot of time helping teachers in their planning, especially of topics, projects and theme work and am often asked what outdoor learning they could 'insert' into their planning for a particular topic they have decided to introduce.

The best outdoor learning is designed as a 'direct experience' activity and I always encourage teachers to see these activities, indoor or outdoor as far more important in the structure of their topic than what 'inserting' might imply. 'Direct experience' offers a foundation for questions, further exploration, a valuable bed of perceptions for cross-curricular follow-up activities and so on. It stimulates the learning process and when well-managed, engages and promotes children's identification with the content.

'Linking back' is a real key to building verticality. It is always helpful to consider a topic in its simplest form, breaking it down into the most fundamental elements. This can take plenty of practice for teachers and the skill to do it is hugely valuable. Once you get back to these foundational 'parts,' you will discover that it is much easier to build a 'direct experience' activity. In this way we 'link back' to a simpler, more basic experience and foster a developing context for deeper learning.

I was asked for example, to help out with a topic the teacher had enthusiastically titled 'Rise of the Robots,' for children of around nine. She thought this would capture their interest, which was the prime reason she gave for choosing the topic. My interest was to find some kind of direct experience which might give such young children a way into the world of robots, which otherwise would simply have encouraged rehashed video game and movie based excitement.

The identifying characteristic I felt the children might most easily grasp, certainly more than artificial intelligence was the engineering of moving parts. Most of this is dependent on leverage of one sort or other and so I suggested planning to explore levers in a simple, tangible way and then going on to build a small, wooden 'toy-robot' complete with moving arms and legs.

We set a problem/task for the class of how to move a series of boulders from one part in the garden to another without getting a contractor in. This inevitably led to many suggested solutions, each of which, as a hypothesis, needed setting out and then testing, with accompanying written and photographic record keeping. Eventually the idea of a lever surfaced, was tried out and with onlookers cheering, one of the boulders was successfully rolled into place. Levers in various forms could then be studied, including our own joints, providing the 'linking back' to robot movement.

With primary school children we are not necessarily looking for *the definitive* link, simply something that for the particular age of child is graspable as a direct experience and which gives them a connection to the topic content.

In a similar way we can explore whole topics or particular parts of content by 'linking back' to earlier, simpler historical forms. This works very well, either as a developmental time-line for children moving from one year to the next through the school or as a way of working through certain activities when introducing them to inexperienced children.

Using the example of robots above, one of the historically related areas we could explore might be the idea of tools as helpers in our work. This will link us all the

86

way back to the digging stick, and depending on the creativity of the teacher, will make for a wonderfully progressive sequence of connected experiences and follow-up school work.

Establishing strong verticality in the outdoor learning programme is essential for its success in the school. We do that by building in regular, eagerly anticipated events into the annual school calendar, allowing for key opportunities to take place where we can integrate meaningful outdoor learning. In addition, when we work with 'linking back' to build progression in the 'direct experience' of content, we emphasise a healthy verticality that connects the curriculum over time. We also need to ensure that there is a similar level of stability in the topic programme taken each year. This does not need in any way to reduce teachers' creativity. Their imaginative and inspirational leadership is fundamental to great schools and the best education.

The Four Keys & the Horizontal Axis

The horizontal axis is the path throughout the year - how the topics and class work are related in such a way that we have a steady progression of skills and knowledge built into the programme. The four keys that I use are:

Key 1:	Level - Knowing your children

Key 2:	Order - Understanding the processes

Key 3:   System - Managing the experience

Key 4:   Closure - Grounding the experience

These areas are also all very closely linked of course, but it helps to be able to focus on particular aspects even though the process involved is best understood as a whole.

Key 1: Level

Getting the *level* right is all about knowing your children and matching the appropriate developmental level in the choices you make. The Cambridge Review, 'the first comprehensive investigation of English primary education in 40 years,' since the 1967 Plowden Enquiry makes these points to do with our latest understandings of cognitive development:

'First, babies and young children learn, think and reason in all the same ways as adults – what they lack is *the experience* to make sense of what they find.'

'Second, their learning depends on the development of multi-sensory networks of neurons *distributed across the whole brain*.'

'Third, children learn from *every experience*, their brains distributing the information across these networks, with stronger 'representations' of what the experiences have in common.'

'Fourth, the biological, social, emotional and intellectual aspects of learning are inextricably interwoven.'

'Fifth, even the most basic learning relies on effective linguistic and social interaction with parents, teachers and other children.'

'Finally, children, like most humans, tend to interpret the world in line with their own explanations as to why things happen.'

Although we know that children's development does not advance in fixed stages, this does not mean it is open season on doing whatever comes to mind and nor does it mean that just because a child can manage to some extent with the support of an adult, that we are constructively bridging the gap between can and can't, Vygotsky's zone of proximal development.

An early years' teacher spoke to me about her class and their forest school experiences. *'My four year olds are doing really well with their fire-making,'* she said. *'They've almost got the friction method now!'*

Have you ever seen a bush-craft expert working with the friction method, bow and drill for example, to make a fire? I have watched a skilled bush-crafter work so hard at it that he drew blisters from his hands. On a good day it requires genuine skill, strength, balance and a great deal of perseverance, let alone the sophisticated level of experience and knowledge to choose the right materials in the first place.

I was not surprised though.

Even sadder than her misreading of her children's experience and the fact that they had even been subject to such an inappropriate set of activities, was the fact that this is not at all uncommon, generally not with kindergarten aged children, but with primary school children certainly. Because their teachers do not know how to use the environment, are themselves unfamiliar with and largely disconnected from it – and also because they so often seek the next new thing to do, they cannot deepen the simplest of experiences, without changing the 'level.'

Young children for example, are guided to use sophisticated forestry tools such as bow-saws. Why? The great temptation our teachers have fallen for, is believing that introducing an activity, skill or concept from a more sophisticated stage of development equals progression.

It may, but it generally doesn't!

It is far better to increase the experience base, adding to the 'representations of what the experiences have in common.' We need to allow children more and more opportunities to experience something from different angles, through artistic, adventurous, scientific, musical, literary eyes, because, 'what they lack is *the experience* to make sense of what they find.' Making sense of what they find is learning. Being told the meaning of what they find is very different. They may well be able to give exam answers, but they have not built the experiences and they do not 'know' through their own, independent, 'development of multi-sensory networks of neurons distributed across the whole brain.'

But in any case, bringing experiences to children too early is simply wasting opportunities for a far more meaningful engagement later. Fire making, for example, has always been a revered skill in traditional communities. It was passed on when the training adolescent was also capable of managing the *social responsibility* that the role carried.

I have known young children suffer nightmares as a result of the intense health and safety warnings they received during their outdoor fire-circle sessions. Because the children are too young for the task, we have to alert them to dangers and insist on their compliance with safety measures, such as, 'Stand back. Don't touch,' when their natural inclination is exactly the opposite - They need to touch and they need to be fully involved in order to experience.

We fill our children with our own fears and at the same time offer them tantalising activities which we don't allow them to engage in properly. They are passive observers. Teachers then go on to explain what is happening in front of them in order to compensate for the children's non participation.

We teach our children how to be bored. Firstly we frustrate them when younger by restricting their genuine participation in the activities we introduce them to. Then, by having already introduced the activity too early, we turn the adolescent off when we try to engage them in something they think they've already done and know, just when their natural tendency is to seek out new and unfamiliar horizons. If we get the level right, we increase the opportunity for children to build a quality of meaning that is appropriate for their own individual stage of development.

Key 2: Order

We can now look a little more closely at what I have called the *preliminary and closing processes*. Our goal is to build a series of experiences which are embedded in the rest of the children's work and which allow the, 'inextricably interwoven...biological, social, emotional and intellectual aspects of learning,' to take root and be expressed. We are looking to *order* the sequence of parts to build an enriched process the children can draw their learning from.

If we recall the earlier descriptions of the psychological meaning of children's play, especially the way critical foundations for meaning are rehearsed, practised and nurtured; we can see how important it is to get the method for delivering outdoor experiences to match the child's natural inclination for learning.

All children are drawn to story, to narrative. They play out scenarios in a story form and intimately link the entire experience with creative and mobile narrative. They are alive in their internal picturing and this mental imagery is remembered as a door back into the experience. They will play the 'game' over and over, adding to and embellishing it each time.

By preparing the children for a particular outdoor activity through story, we match their learning predisposition. Even when a teacher describes in very practical terms what is going to happen, the children will be trying unconsciously to take it in as a story. But when it has no imagery, no story structure, it is easily forgotten by many. They will rely on copying others to know what to do when they eventually go outside.

A simple, alternative method is to 'plant the seeds of the activity' in story-form some days before. It works well to repeat the story, possibly from a different point of view on the next day. The younger the children, the more 'fairy-tale' the style of story, mentioning a special task the little bear has to complete, mirroring what you'll be asking the children to do. You can spend a little more time describing in detail key landmarks, times, and boundaries in the story, creating a structural landscape in images which you will 'use' later.

There is no need for explanation, but it helps very much to work on aspects of the story together, drawing the great tree or recalling the order of unfolding events for example. For older children, the subject matter you are studying at the time - history, science, English and so on - will give you the 'story' content. Look for biographies of people who have worked on the areas you'll be exploring. Even an anecdote, perhaps of your own experience will work in this way. It is the manner of delivery that lends the content its story-like quality and prepares the way for the following outdoor activity.

To make the experience more immediate, telling rather than reading the 'story' is a very powerful tool. It takes a little practice but as it is not a performance, the children, regardless of age are very forgiving. One of the reasons it works so well is because, in order to communicate the images in the story, the story-teller must first create a version of those images in h/er own mind's eye. The more vibrant the story-teller's internal imagery, the more vibrant is the image then created by the listener.

When you work with oral narrative, you are able to be flexible with managing both the story content and the social experience. You can highlight specific images you want the children to be aware of, drawing out the perceptions, deepening the pictures. If you paint the images vividly, they will be drawn to those experiences when outdoors. This practice enhances the networking we are always doing, finding links and connections between the new perceptions and what we already 'know.'

We not only form a bridge between the images and the practical outdoor experience; we also draw out the potential for an image which might have attracted a particular child's attention, to lead to something more personal. The metaphorical quality of an experience is enhanced when that child combines what they have created as a picture from your story with a special moment they feel when outdoors.

We enhance the children's sense of discovery, making that experience even more memorable if we prepare the foundations ahead of time for them to bridge, for them to make their own connections.

Following the activity, we are then able to continue by having the children recall the experience as a discussion group. Piecing together what happened and in what order before you look for explanations is hugely helpful for everyone. This is the beginning of the next step in the sequence - the *interpretive experience.* You will see then if the 'seeds' you planted have helped the children notice and perceive more acutely. There is a wide range of classroom based activities which you can use to develop the recollection: listing, recounting, drawing, modelling, interpreting through drama, music, art and so on.

You can then begin to explore the ideas that have come up through the children's responses, answers to questions, explanations to mysteries. With their involvement, further investigations can be developed, based on unanswered puzzles or where disagreement and uncertainty are evident.

Working through a thorough interpretive experience builds confidence in the process. It forms children's habits for concluding work, knowing what is known, agreeing and accepting what is not and taking real responsibility for their learning and the learning process.

Key 3: System

There are many elements in the *system* of managing the experience, but I want to focus here on one key aspect as it is so different to the way most teachers work. After accomplishing the basics of having the children 'in hand,' the first thing to practise is for them to be able to remain quiet for increasing periods of time. This allows them to observe without interruption.

For children who are trained to answer questions quickly and who want to be acknowledged by their teacher constantly, it can take some time to help them learn how to control their impulse to respond. For many of them it is a hangover from when they were younger. They are accustomed to having their requests met immediately.

Similarly, children tend now to be free to confer constantly. They feel insecure being 'alone,' so it is a step that needs practising. Outdoor learning always begins with learning *how* to be outdoors. We are teaching them how to engage. It can take time, but it will make a huge difference to the school culture.

There is much more to be learned by observing, than what jumps out at the children at first glance. In fact it's the skill of observation itself which is the most important outcome. Their senses need support and their perceptions need sharpening. Anytime we can help them differentiate their first impressions into more detailed observations, the more we help the development of their higher thinking skills.

They will certainly need positive recognition, so help them to hold back speedy judgements by having them try to describe rather than explain. This practice allows more complex networking to take place. As we build up the habit of interpretation based on genuine observation, we encourage them to begin their questioning on a much more informed basis. We give them the language for this level of question formation through our own modelling of the method.

As a teacher, you also have to practise holding back. The first thing most of us want to do is to answer children's spontaneous questions. It is much better however, to guide and extend their thinking. A quick answer, even if it is expected content, tends to seal off the child's continuing thought and confirms to them that such an answer is *the answer*. It takes a lot of reorientation by a teacher who is so accustomed to firing off answers all day - but it is one of the most productive changes s/he can do to increase higher order thinking in the class.

Key 4: Closure

Grounding the experience, giving it a place in the learning map is the final step in the process. This is the area of *closure*. Our understanding of the interpretive experience contributes very much to this step. We want the children to *order and articulate* what they have experienced, appropriate to their *level*.

We also want the potential for networking these experiences to be as rich as possible.

It is critical that we encourage them to express their work through as wide a set of media forms as is also possible.

They need to engage with the content through the eyes of a scientist, a painter, a sculptor, an author, a journalist, an actor and so on. This breadth of expression is what develops the network of 'what the experiences have in common.' Because 'the biological, social, emotional and intellectual aspects of learning are inextricably interwoven,' this is what makes sense of school. We look at our own experiences, no matter how young and little we are, through our cultural senses. This is creative learning – where outdoors and indoors are also inextricably interwoven.

Four Whole-School Elements

Four interrelating parts of a complex, communal puzzle need to function really well together for the development of an integrated, working *whole-school outdoor learning culture*.

Element 1: Children

Element 2: Home

Element 3: Nature

Element 4: Teachers

Element 1: Children

When children's personal and social development are central to the school's ethos, and both are successfully catered for in practice, the whole community responds in support of what it is trying to do. Parents notice changes in their children's motivation. Children, who are enthusiastic about projects, will tend to talk about what they are doing and want to share it with others. By creating a culture of engagement we bring about a greater community school spirit as parents and teachers recognise changes in the children's excitement and interest. Their enthusiasm carries the school forward.

Managing the school community in such a way that it adjusts confidently in line with the evolving ethos takes real initiative and great professional skill by school leaders. But the foundation for any progress is the children's well-being and that is dependent on us matching how we teach with how they most naturally learn.

Many writers agree that the 'window' for truly connecting with nature and forming positive attitudes towards the environment develops during early to middle childhood. Kellert (2002) for example, describes a special moment he calls an 'imprint,' that occurs somewhere in 'middle childhood,' between six and twelve years old - a life-altering nature-experience, which creates a lasting impression, and continues to influence the experience of self and nature thereafter.

I had one of those; my special 'ditch' experience. I grew up in the Australian outback, a mining settlement, vast open countryside of iron-stone and dry, red dirt. In the heat of the day one afternoon, I found myself sitting at the bottom of a small cutting, perhaps only as deep as a man and as wide as his arms outstretched, on the edge of the track we called the main-road-into-town. It was cool and shaded down at the bottom and I was there for a long time, digging and scratching at the levels of colour in the cliff-like banks on either side. Layer upon layer of fine, dry colour ran in lines along the wall, ochres of red, yellow, blue-grey and white.

I carved out small piles of every shade I could find until the floor was covered, like a palette of earthen paint powders. Of course, at that age I had no idea of the wonders of geomorphology that create such a world of ancient sedimentary layering; but I felt the wonder of it. I had seen a rainbow once, majestic in the sky after a desert storm had arched above our little town and poured down a year's supply in a matter of minutes. I called these layers my earth-rainbow.

I never went there again and having gone off to boarding school in the city several hundred miles south on the coast, forgot about it altogether, When I did finally recall the experience as an adult many years later, I realised how hugely important that day and those feelings had been in forming the way I understood life and nature. It was as if, in those moments with the intricate seams of coloured earth I had wakened a deep sense for the connectedness of everything.

Children's inner imaginative experience accompanies the outer manipulation of natural materials. Creating fairy houses, building dens, running, exploring, collecting, chasing and hiding games – the psychology of these archetypal childhood experiences is not so difficult to grasp. But to recognise that everything a child does has this potential is another step. The simplest moment may well be *that* moment. It has nothing to do with how long it takes and everything to do with being in the right place, doing the right thing in the right moment.

Children's unconscious dreams of becoming the person they really are - the prince, the princess, the hero – are so easily diverted by the glittering treasures promised for the rich and famous, the media and sporting celebrities living the high life. Ask young teenagers where the line is that they will cross to pass into adulthood and they generally tell you one of two things: getting their driver's licence or being able to drink! Ask children what they want to become as adults and they'll commonly say it's all to do with wealth and fame.

We help them to reconnect, not only to nature but to themselves when we get the levels right in what we teach and when we teach it, what experiences we encourage and when we encourage them. It makes all the difference. We give them opportunities to develop personally and socially based on genuine interaction with others, themselves and the environment – their work. We encourage the qualities which Goleman says represent emotional intelligence: trustworthiness responsibility, respect, fairness, caring, citizenship and so on:

'There is an old fashioned word for the body of skills that emotional intelligence represents: Character.'

You cannot teach character. It is forged through the challenges of life experience. But we can help to lay the foundations for it. The idea that characteristics such as honesty, resilience and perseverance are 'skills' to be learned has not been helpful. The last thing we want is a child with a skill for being honest.

At primary school level, we can see the foundations of emerging character in two areas – empathy and integrity – a feeling for others and a feeling for self. Personal and social awareness around the end of middle childhood is mobile, easily influenced and gradually gaining definition. Sensitively designed, experiential outdoor learning has a great deal to offer at this stage of their development.

Element 2: Home

I have worked with parents for over twenty five years, helping them to understand that their children's lifestyles are a key determinant in how they engage in their learning. We all know that our schools need to build an on-going, working relationship with the parent community. By creating a whole-school outdoor learning culture, we have a wonderful opportunity to reach out and involve parents, many who have otherwise remained on the periphery.

Although head teachers are often tempted to seize upon projects such as building an outdoor learning classroom to motivate parent fund-raising and hands-on involvement, this drives schools towards a financial rather than a social and learning investment. It is far better to look at offers of time and skill-sharing by parents which translate directly into constructive, down-to-earth activity with the children.

Just as we need a lot of home support for successful literacy programmes in school, we also need the same level of support for the children's ability to engage. One of these is providing them with rich opportunities to play outdoors, explore outdoors and learn to love the outdoors. Parents are beginning to see that supporting more natural and simple forms of play has huge benefits.

The school/home alliance needs to make this its central focus, so that together we can encourage children's out-of-school development in as positive a way as possible. It is of enormous help to parents if they understand what it is we are trying to achieve. Mostly this doesn't happen by talking about it or writing newsletters. It happens best, for most adults by doing it, being a part of it. Reaching out in this way to the parent community is an essential and integral part of building the whole-school culture.

We are all part of bigger social pressures and it is really important to work together to enable children to make the most of opportunities we are trying to create in our schools. Just as we teachers need to make sure they are in the right frame of mind, the right readiness to engage with the outdoor learning, so parents can help hugely by supporting this 'readiness' too.

Many adults are in real conflict with how they deal with children. It is the same for teachers, often parents themselves as it is for the parents in our schools. They find themselves in a continual 'negotiation trap' with their children and the behaviour this encourages plays into the way the children are able to relate to learning through experience and the natural environment as much as to other children and adults they have to deal with.

For one reason or another, we have taught our children to haggle with us over almost everything possible – from what and when to eat, to the type of video games they have and how much they use them. We have exchanged the old fashioned 'Do-as-I-say' parenting style with what we hoped would be a more reasoned, civilised approach, teaching our children, through practice, how best to get on with each other, cooperatively negotiating their way through life's predicaments.

And how has it left us? This is typical - an everyday struggle between five year old Lucas and his mother:

Lucas: *I hate beans. I can't eat them.*

Mother: *You need to eat three bites.*

Lucas: (whining) *I can't eat three bites. I'll throw up.*

Mother: *That's fine. Just eat three bites.*

Lucas: (a minute later) *There, I'm done.*

Mother: *You're not done. You didn't eat three bites.*

Lucas: (bursting with denial) *I did too! They were small.*

Mother: *That won't do it.*

Lucas: *All right, three beans. I already ate one.*

Mother: *I said three bites.*

Lucas: *That is three bites. They're big.*

Mother: *They're beans.*

Lucas: *If I eat three beans, how many M&Ms can I have?*

Mother: *I don't know.*

Lucas: *Twenty?*

Mother: *No, you haven't eaten enough.*

Lucas: *I ate all my apple sauce and all my bread!*

105

Mother: *All right, ten M&M's.*

Mother: *Fifteen.*

Mother: *I said ten.*

Lucas: *If I finish my milk, can I have fifteen?*

Mother: *OK, but bring your plate to the kitchen.*

From Scott Brown's book: *How to Negotiate With Kids Even When You Think You Shouldn't*

Lucas has well and truly begun to win the battle with his mother. In fact, he has simply worn her down. This interaction is only the tip of the mountain of course, a mountain they have been building together for a long time. It's now so big Mum can't imagine how she could ever get over it. It's just too big to deal with. She's tired and worn out and Lucas is leading the negotiation. He knows when to ask a question, when to complain, when to be silent and of course, when to wait it out.

I have often asked children after observing similar interactions with their parents, '*Is it worth the trouble?*'

'*Oh sure,*' comes the reply. '*It works at least once or twice every few times.*' That's good odds, roughly 1 in 4. You realise pretty quickly that children, like so many of us, are out to get what they want if they can.

What has happened for us to feel so insecure, so often in our roles as adults and as parents? A different meal for each child in the family? A TV in each child's bedroom? Bed times always a battle? Getting homework and simple clearing up done, a traumatic conflict of wills?

A cocktail of social and economic change has meant that the way we see our children and ourselves is very different from a 'traditional' style of parenting. We want to see our children as individuals, participating equally in their own development, with a natural tendency for knowing what is best for themselves. We like our children to talk with us more, connecting on a more adult level.

We tend to see more verbal, interactive children as more intelligent children, mistaking precociousness for maturity. Although it is confusing and dispiriting to have our children talk back to us, arguing and bargaining for what they want, we never-the-less encourage it as a strange sign of equality.

Once childhood was recognised as a period of development with its own integrity, our bias has always been to bring down from the older age group into the younger ages what doesn't necessarily belong there. Because children appear to be 'aux fait' with a more adult world, it does not mean that they can manage that world, or that the challenges to their well-being are only that they have to cope intellectually. Children suffer emotionally when they have to carry the responsibilities and burdens which are ours, as adults. Too much choice, too young, shifts parenting responsibilities onto their shoulders as we look for an indication in their reactions for what might be the next 'right' step to choose.

Unfortunately the challenges we face in our relationships with our children are as much a part of the wider commercialisation of childhood as they are of our own particular struggles as parents. There has been an enormous explosion of marketing to children based on the psychology of knowing how children are most easily influenced. Advertisers take important cultural realities and work them for their own purposes. As a result, children have been systematically empowered to take control in their families.

Growing up has always meant struggling with the challenges of self-awareness, separating from parents and adults in general. Marketers work to exaggerate these feelings, creating a special, cool 'kid's world' opposed to the boring, old fashioned world of the adults.

To drive a wedge between the adult and child helps to release a new buying power. Children are gaining an ever greater control over their parents' salaries and this increase in independently spent income amounts to an estimated global buying power of around £7 billion per year in direct sales and £15 billion in sales affected by children, such as at least 65% of car purchases the industry estimates is down to the children's choice of vehicle.

So while we are losing faith in the carrot and the stick, wanting them to discuss with us in a rational way whether they should be at the sleep-over when the parents are away for the week-end or if the content of a particular computer game is age appropriate, the children are becoming ever more skilled at the negotiation game, manipulating adversaries. Who can blame them?

They learn to become resilient. 'I don't care what you do,' can leave us feeling helpless. Perhaps they'll just wait until we are busy. Years of knowing how we will manage a situation and years of us talking to them about it, means that they know the language and the ways of reversing the roles. When all else fails there is always the threat of embarrassment in front of our friends, or more publicly in the school car park and the supermarket. By teaching our children to negotiate with us too much, too soon, we teach them to barter, to horse-trade. We teach them the lowest form of negotiation – what do I get out of it? We limit what we are trying, in the end, to achieve.

Raising children is a process and as children develop, the process has to develop. What's good for an older child is not necessarily good for a younger one. Being able to negotiate is a very good thing but it too needs a sense of development and we need to be thinking about how our children can learn to relate to others in a gradual and progressive way. As parents, it is helpful if we understand that constructive, creative negotiation is supported by wisdom born out of experience.

Schools can do an enormous amount to support parents in this process as well. Far too often teachers see parents as the root of behaviour problems which they have to deal with in the school environment. It is an unsophisticated judgement to make and is not surprisingly shared by some of those parents themselves about their children's teachers. Although it may be difficult to manage challenging behaviours, blaming parents does nothing to bring about positive change.

Where teachers have this attitude, it is not usually confined just to the most difficult of relationships. It can be a view shared, by the staff room of parents in general. Having a closer look, together with parents, at modern family relationships, ways to raise children and the pressures we all find ourselves under in information and discussion evenings, setting aside specific times to meet parents and carers when they can actually make those times, being proactive about establishing working relationships and making certain that everyone's engagement is valued – these are the kind of initiative-taking steps which communicate clearly that a school and its teachers are interested in the home. It shows that the teachers are prepared to support parents and that they see collaboration between school and home is vitally important for a child's education.

Element 3: Nature

Thinking of nature, usually conjures idyllic scenes, often a forest, birds singing or a pastoral, rural setting full of peace and tranquillity. Is this how we imagine school grounds? Nature like this, is a little like higher order thinking. It is highly sophisticated, mature, complex and has a long evolution leading to its particular level of expression.

School grounds don't normally offer nature like this. They are lucky if they have trees and bushes, let alone meadow. The only grass is normally mown regularly by contractors who sweep in on large machinery, give everything in sight a 'short back and sides,' and then drive away to the next school in order to cram in as many jobs as possible in a day. The grassed area is then either commandeered by the older boys as their football pitch or ruled 'out-of-bounds,' as it is waterlogged and too muddy to play on.

Wooded areas, including hedges have always been thought of as the kind of place children are likely to hide in, away from prying adults eyes and there get up to mischief. On my walk-a-bouts with the head teacher and staff, having a closer look at the grounds and the grounds' development during training sessions, I always take them to the boundaries of the playground to see what has been taking place in the peace there.

The lone bush generally has signs of significant wear around its base, particularly on the 'blind' side, where the children who meet there are screened from the adults watching over them. They will usually be the older girls, getting away, in order to talk secretly amongst themselves.

Look around the far reaches of the playground for evidence of the quiet worker, an almost-extinct-endangered-species, to see how s/he has been searching for that hidden, out-of-sight, quiet place to 'get on with the job.' Note the signs of digging and carving in the

hardened pile of earth, left behind after 'building improvements' or piled up as part of the landscaping. The 'scratchers and diggers' have been at work.

These are the children who are still playing, by creating small-world fairy gardens, patterns in the dirt, car tracks and dolly houses. They are usually over-run by the streaming 'fire engines' racing about, whooping and hollering during break time and so they escape as far away as they are able, to places where they can catch their breath.

School-yard playgrounds were and still are dominated by their overriding role as places of observation. Instead of allowing for and encouraging expansive, exploratory play, they inhibit children's natural tendencies and foster sports-based running and ball games.

We still have the majority of primary school children taking their 'break time' in fenced, flat, hard-paved, tarmac-covered areas adjacent to the school buildings where playground assistants are most easily able to oversee their play. Critically, the design is intended to reduce the number of observers to a minimum, allowing also for their actual involvement to be reduced to a minimum and all this while holding a cup of coffee. This is the environment which has carefully cultivated the 'teacher shriek'!

These factors affect the nature of children's engagement, both with the play itself and also with others, either involved in the game or simply within the immediate environment. The design criteria are not set for the benefit of the children but for the teachers and others who are watching over them.

Another long-held view still dominating playground design and the use of play areas in schools, is the idea that the purpose of play is to 'burn off energy' - particularly so with boys. Although this idea is still prevalent amongst teachers, contributing to all sorts of problems in expectations and associated behaviour issues, it is in fact based on a misreading of children's needs.

The playground and the school's grounds in general, play a major part in the way children socialise and therefore form a sense of identity. They are far from simply being a physical place. They involve time, activity, people and the views about what takes place there, how it takes place, what should and should not take place and also the value of what takes place.

So how does 'nature' have a part to play?

A teacher attending a training course I was running told me about her school's plans to create a nature trail in the woody copse they were lucky to have on the school grounds. It was to have paths, name-signs on the trees and suggestions for learning activities. Another spoke about how her school had developed their playground to include some 'natural elements' - a large balancing log, some painted nature pictures on the hard surfaces and a bird table.

Heads and teachers often see these features as signs of outdoor learning. In fact many schools have the ol' willow tunnel out there somewhere in their grounds, usually near the other 'required' outdoor learning artefacts, the raised veggie beds, the 'bug hotels' and the 'outdoor classroom!'. Of course there's nothing wrong with willow tunnels per se, but unfortunately there is a problem with the expectation many teachers have or have been sold, that somehow willow tunnel + children = outdoor learning or that nature trail + children = outdoor learning.

Clearly this problem doesn't really have anything to do with willow tunnels any more than it does with painted nature pictures, raised garden beds, bird boxes or any of the paraphernalia we see scattered about the edges of the school grounds. None of these so-called 'outdoor learning' requirements + children = outdoor learning. The real essence of what can be achieved and what genuine value can be gained from taking *school* children during *school* time into the *school* grounds has been lost by teachers who have missed what is absolutely crucial:

Nature is not an 'add-on.' It is not something 'over there.' You can't point at or direct attention to it. Trees are not nature. Birds are not nature. It is the life energy of our planet and we are all an intimate part of it. It exists even in the school grounds where tarmac covers the whole area. Watch and wait and the evidence will begin to show.

The best way to get closer to nature is to be creative. And the best way for children to be creative springs from their play.

Sir Ken Robinson, in his best-selling and hugely influential book, *Out of Our Minds, Learning to be Creative* takes the view that, *'The dominant forms of education actively stifle the conditions that are essential to creative development.'* He points to the connection between imagination, creativity and innovation and makes an excellent case for our 21st century education system needing to refocus its aims to include creativity at its centre.

We have a fantastic opportunity to give depth and foundation to children's learning through experience by encouraging them to engage creatively and artistically with the natural elements we find in our school environment.

Most schools do not have a piece of woodland but they do have access to natural elements – earth, water, fire and air – the same elements our ancestors learned how to use, to manipulate and to create with. These are the elements children discover in their play. It is our job to extend their play into their work.

There is a very wide list of possibilities for the uses of earth, mud, clay and stone, for example. If we begin with the simplest, most naive forms of play, such as digging, scratching, creating fairy gardens, making mud figures, we can gradually introduce levels of sophistication according to the content of the other work the children are doing. Because their imagination is so vivid, the representation of houses, villages, boats or castles can be rudimentary. If we call it a house, it is a house.

The important thing is that the children are engaged in the creative activity using natural elements. Similarly, we can begin to introduce technological developments like pottery, which itself has a long history we can 'mine,' building up over a long period of time from the most primitive methods to those that are highly refined. Many art teachers have built simple earth kilns, raku kilns and even larger brick and clay kilns. For the primary school, there are very simple ways to introduce appropriate, creative, integrated outdoor learning experiences, which evolve progressively, 'link back' within topics and which the children will love and benefit from.

It is ideal of course, to have school grounds which are more developed and which provide woods and meadows. Even very small areas can be used productively. But instead of hiring in expensive contractors or buying plants which may well not survive, there are simpler, more down-to-earth ways of working with children to make the changes.

The first action is to control the mowing regime. Work out exactly what needs to be mown and for what purpose. Then you can look at golf courses for inspiration – introduce several 'cuts' in an ordered 'grass-scape,' leaving the borders to grow up wild and mature. They can then all be cut together, giving plenty of hay for den building, ready for the next cycle. These differentiated cuts allow sports and ball games to combine with free, creative play. Because children can run in and out of the longer grass, they will lose far fewer balls than you will find floating in the fenced, out-of-bounds pond area.

Where you want to encourage trees and bushes to grow, it makes much better educational sense to look at the 'whole cycle' for your activity. Normally, tree saplings turn up at the school, ordered by a teacher. Children are then organised to 'help' with the planting. If we start from the beginning however, by looking at what grows, how it grows, why it grows, we can cover an enormous amount of content with real 'roots.'

If a hedge is planned, explore hedges together. Make 'hedges' a project. Find a good one and 'discover' it from every school work, skill type angle you have – drawing, photographs, history, poetry, botany and so on. Can you take cuttings, seeds? Can you create a hedge? How?

Working on a 'roots' project like this helps the children to create rich internal connections. New information links to what they have experienced. It becomes memorable.

As we become more creative with the natural *elements* in our school environment, we encourage more and more *nature* to show itself – we can then observe it, record it, study the plant types, the increase in butterflies and worms, the number and size of trees, the nests and the baby birds – all because we start slowly, paying close attention to the roots of what we do and looking for a creative engagement at all times:

You cannot have any distance between the child and the experience.

You cannot buy in an outdoor learning culture.

Element 4: Teachers

The first tool to learn in the teacher's tool kit is *how to observe, how to notice.* So often teachers are full of what they are preparing, rushing from one thing to the next, cramming coffee and handling several things at once.

When I finally realised, at one point in my teaching, that I was finding children's questions and their attempts to speak to me at the beginning of breaks annoying and interruptive, I had to have a very close look at what was more important – their questions and need for attention or my need for a cigarette and another coffee. I decided right then to quit, in the moment I realised what was happening. I didn't need any other motivation. The frightening thing I also realised was that it had been going on for some time. I simply had not recognised it. Something so obvious had escaped my attention, wrapped up in my own habits and needs as I was.

I was certainly not alone and as I tour the country visiting schools, I see exactly the same thing happen time after time – perfectly sincere, well-meaning and talented teachers ignoring and passing over children's attempts to communicate.

We have even institutionalised the practice by having playground staff monitoring the break times. At the most important time to be observing children - at their play - we have passed over the opportunity to others so that we can have a hot drink, take a break and rush on to the next task.

'Reading' children through their behaviour is a key skill for teachers and it allows us to not only assess competencies but it also gives an insight into the way they interact socially and with their environment through play.

Once we are aware of where the children are 'up to' with their independent activity, knowing what the children are doing in the playground, opens up genuine possibilities for introducing similar activities. We can begin to model aspects of the school work on these insights.

Another source of material we can use to encourage real engagement is to connect the children's work to whatever is actually going on around them. This means that teachers also need to notice changes, not only in the children themselves but in the environment – simple changes – the weather, the seasons, the plants, the builders next door, the flooded creek at the bottom of the school, the number of children away with 'flu. Using this world of 'here & now' brings a sense of vitality to their work, a feeling that they are actually learning about something real and relevant.

When we learn to notice the subtle changes that are taking place in nature, we can use these changes in the class work. Notice the myriad spider webs in early autumn, for example, covering everything in the early morning. Watch the spiders at work, meticulously weaving, following an innate pattern, picking off the sections of the process one bit at a time, systematic, methodical.

By drawing out the children's observation, their ability to describe, their developing artistic and creative responses, we can use this natural urge in the children's work. Systematic, methodical patterns – tidying up and focusing on book work, hand writing, working number patterns, tables, reorganizing kit. Help them to have something to feel proud of and something the important adults in their lives will feel proud of too.

Nature provides a never-ending source of inspiration and metaphor which we can learn first to notice and then to use. A simple method such as this creates immediacy and fosters engagement. But it also works deeply to connect children to nature and the world around them and contributes enormously to their ability to understand themselves and the world as they grow up.

When we, as teachers, feel a sense of wonder in the marvels of nature, we offer our classes an inspirational role model.

This is deepened and made real by our own efforts at actual observation, by getting our hands dirty, going outside ourselves and really looking, noticing and building our own experience.

We don't need to know names, orders, scientific categories. We simply have to model the behaviour we would like to encourage. Go out exploring. Collect stuff you notice and find interesting. Bring it in to the classroom. You'll have two things the children will be really keen to learn about: Your story – what you did, where you went, what you saw – and then, the actual thing you found. Your story will fill it with interest and will encourage the children to do the same.

Wrapping Up

A whole-school *culture* for outdoor learning, as I am describing it, is much more than doing some outdoor learning work with the children. Because it is whole-school and community based, it will shape and define the school's identity. Because it relies on the emerging creativity of teachers and engages the creative spirit of the children it will shape and define the people who are at the heart the school. And because it is woven into the whole of the fabric of the teaching and learning it will shape and define the nature of the education in the school.

In a nutshell:

Outdoor learning is *not* a subject - it is an opportunity, a window into a method.

Outdoor learning is part of a much wider *experience-based learning.*

It offers us a way to *build the foundations for creativity* for all children, not just those we believe to be 'talented.'

Genuine outdoor learning does not work as an *add-in.*

The best people to work with children *in school environments* are their teachers, not bought-in 'experts.'

The whole-school culture starts with the teachers' confidence, imagination and ability to work with children's *experience of what is real and present.*

Teaching-from-a-child's-experience *needs training in a methodology and creativity.*

Schools need to focus on *sound education* rather than 'saving the planet.'

Outdoor learning education requires a stable vertical and horizontal structure.

It needs to progress children's learning according to a developmentally appropriate understanding.

As I write, I am reminded of so many wonderful adventures I have been a part of with the children I have had the pleasure of teaching. And although there are mountain journeys, limestone kiln creations, gypsy wagon treks and fabulous outdoor plays to share, I thought I would finish with something very much simpler.

I had thirty two young children in my class as a young and inexperienced teacher. Every step forward I knew the children were teaching me how to teach them far more than I was teaching them how to be taught. I struggled to manage their effervescent behaviour at the best of times and my own reactions at the worst! Thank goodness they all seemed to run down the path as eagerly as ever each morning after being dropped off at school.

I had them all day, every day except for one or two lessons and I needed them to catch up with myself and get my breath back. In the afternoons it was all up to me to keep them busy and working. Of course, by this time I was tired and so were they. We were all a little too grumpy and as the children started to rub each other up the wrong way, I knew I had to pull myself together and get things back on track.

One lunch time, after they had eaten and were out at play, I had a moment of inspiration. I ran to my car, jumped in and drove away, not as you may be thinking, drove away and kept on driving – actually, I drove to the nearest shop. I bought a couple of loaves of sliced bread, a pound of butter and a pot of jam.

When I returned to class, I was very pleased. I had a plan and I knew it would work. After our art class I let them out for an afternoon break and went out with them. While they were running about in their games, I began to collect some twigs and an armful of sticks.

By this time I had gathered quite a group of interested children around me, wanting to know what I was doing. I was beginning to grasp something of the art of getting their attention. I also held it for much longer by remaining rather mysterious about my plans.

I made a little pile of the twigs and then went and brought out a small table to set down near the pile. I laid the bread, butter and jam out on the table with a plate and three knives. Now the children were more than interested. But when I took out a box of matches and carefully set light to the little mound of kindling and sticks, they were ready to follow me anywhere!

I had a long, thin stick with a little sharpened fork at the end and I began to toast a piece of bread, holding it over the flames. The smell of the buttered toast and jam brought them all around the fire in a quiet, eager group. As I was the creator, it was my fire. I could welcome the children in and control the way they were to act. I learned a great deal that day: A moment of inspiration can work wonders, but only if you act. To have the children 'in the palm of your hand' means you have to lead them. You have to catch their interest and eagerness for learning and they will follow.

Every day after that for a couple of weeks, I bought the sliced bread, the butter and the jam. And every day after that the afternoons rolled along smoothly. The most important lesson I learned however, was not about being able to lead or how to create interest. That was hugely significant for me at the time. It gave me an opening, a small door which I began to get better and better at opening.

In fact, the most important thing I learned was by watching the rest of the children at play while we cooked the toast, ate together and learned about the fire. I noticed that those who had either finished eating or who had chosen not to have any, were playing together differently. There were fewer squabbles. Their play was more constructive. They managed longer and were happier while they went about their business.

Why was that? Because it wasn't only the children who were involved directly in the activity who were getting on better. The children who were *indirectly* involved were getting on better too. I began to see how my mood and my attitudes affected the children much more deeply than I had thought. What they did, how they behaved and how they played was also influenced by how I felt.

It was as if they showed *outwardly* what I experienced inwardly.

The best outdoor learning does not cost the earth but it does take some work. Creating a whole-school outdoor learning culture is like personal development for a school and as with most things that take work, especially work to do with changing ourselves, we'd probably prefer to look the other way. Schools, heads and teachers will tend to find all sorts of ways to look like they are doing outdoor learning but without any of the 'personal development' necessary.

In the end, the goal is to support the children. This means supporting *their* personal and *their* social development. So it also means that we have to make the same focus – we have to work on ourselves and our schools. We have to work on *our* personal and *our* social development, so we can deliver the right experiences in the right way. Adding anything more to the 'mix,' only increases the pressures on the teachers and ultimately on the children. Life is already too busy for most. We need a simple solution that simplifies school. We need to reconnect education with life and children with education.

Experiential, outdoor learning has the potential to enable this to happen but it needs imaginative leadership and creative practice. You might not choose to do it. Anything less than taking up the entire challenge will only nibble at the edges of that potential. Start with the teaching. Everything else will flow from this.

Appendix 1.

Example Outdoor Learning Policy

Vision, rationale and aims

Outdoor learning is central to providing experience-based education in primary school settings for children. By organising and improving the use of grounds, buildings and local areas, schools create additional and beneficial teaching and learning resources. The outdoor environment can provide settings for learning that are different to but complement learning indoors.

The Learning Outside the Classroom (LOtC) Manifesto, launched in 2006 states: *We believe that every young person should experience the world beyond the classroom as an essential part of learning and personal development, whatever their age, ability or circumstances.*

In 2008, an Ofsted Report into learning outside the classroom highlighted the positive benefits and impact on raising achievement. In its key findings section, it pointed out that: *When planned and implemented well, learning outside the classroom contributed significantly to raising standards and improving pupils' personal, social and emotional development.*

At *(school name)* we believe that all children have the right to experience the unique and special nature of being outdoors. We are committed to enabling our children to use the outside environment as a stimulating learning context wherever possible throughout the year.

Aims:

To enable all children to benefit from the experience of learning outdoors

To integrate outdoor learning throughout the teaching and learning across all year groups

To provide a safe, stimulating and enriching environment in the school grounds

To encourage children to care for their environment

To encourage close links with parents and the school in celebrating our outdoor space and the rich learning that can take place within it.

Planning

The school *(school name)* sees outdoor learning as an important teaching and learning method rather than as a subject in itself. It is integrated into planning wherever appropriate to support learning and provide opportunities to encourage engagement.

Outdoor learning is an experience-based process.

The younger the child, the more the activity will resemble play.

The most successful outdoor learning will be integrated into a wide range of associated learning activities, indoors and outdoors, often project-based.

Outdoor experiences are often better remembered and better assimilated by children. Natural light, more open space and a green, living background provide a more conducive learning environment for them.

Some children can access traditional school work more easily simply by being in an outdoor environment.

Learning about the natural environment is an aspect of learning in a natural environment.

Being active in caring for nature in simple, engaging ways – growing plants, tending animals – is the most productive way of establishing sustainable environmentalism.

Key outdoor learning opportunities are highlighted in teachers' planning.

Teachers are expected to provide frequent and regular experiences for their classes outdoor.

These experiences are expected to be integrated into the rest of the children's school work, making the preparation and follow up for these experiences more worthwhile in the learning process and more memorable for the children.

In general, the younger the year group, the more often they are outdoors. Scheduling reflects this pattern.

Because the outdoor learning opportunities are best when they are part of an integrated topic, timetabling for those opportunities depend on each teacher's planning rather than as designated lessons or time allocations in the timetable.

Roles and Responsibilities

A designated teacher, *(i.e. Head of Outdoor Learning, HOL)* oversees the development and management of the school's outdoor learning and supports teachers' ability to deliver the aims of the school.

This means:

Ensuring teachers have the necessary knowledge and skills.

Being aware of and providing suitable training opportunities.

Monitoring planning to ensure it is both relevant and adequate.

Checking on delivery to ensure it meets school aims.

Overseeing equipment needs.

Following up opportunities for whole-school outdoor learning celebrations.

The designated teacher liaises with:

(Include here a list of people the designated teacher is expected to liaise with to fulfil her/his role, such as:)

<u>The School Health & Safety Officer</u> so that outdoor learning experiences in the school are conducted safely and the school grounds provide a stimulating but safe

environment for outdoor teaching and learning. *(refer Appendix D: School Health & Safety policy)*

<u>Ground Staff</u> to support school grounds' development.

<u>Senior Management</u> to ensure the necessary framework is in order for outdoor learning aims to be met. This includes:

Assessment *(refer Appendix B – School Assessment & Evaluation Policy)*

Integration with other related school development policies *(refer Appendix C - School Development Policy)*

Inclusion *(refer Appendix E – School Equal Opportunities Policy)*

Finance

Observation, Assessment, Monitoring, Evaluation

Observation and assessment, monitoring and evaluation of outdoor learning progress are clearly linked to the aims and requirements set out in points 2 & 3 above.

Evidence is collected by teachers from children's outdoor learning related school work in a variety of different ways. The HOL collates evidence regularly to provide a foundation for establishing and improving progression.

Termly opportunities are made for the HOL to:

View teachers' medium term planning.

Collect and collate evidence from children's outdoor learning related school work.

Report to senior management on outdoor learning progress across all year groups and for the whole-school.

Recommend to senior management where further training is required, equipment needs provision and school grounds could be improved.

(Refer Appendix B: School Assessment & Evaluation Policy)

Outdoor Learning Resources

<u>Outdoor Classroom</u>: *(Include arrangements for use of the outdoor classroom here. Refer Appendix 2 Outdoor Classrooms; A Growing Convention.)*

<u>Future Development</u>: The school's Grounds' Development Plan *(Section of School Development Plan)* is set out in several phases:

Phase 1 (2012/13)

Phase 2 (2013/14)

The following future phase is recommended: Phase 3

(See Appendix C: School Development Plan; ensure outdoor learning focus/grounds improvement etc. are included.)

<u>Outdoor Clothing</u>: (Schools tend to have their own arrangements for wet-weather clothing. These need to be clearly outlined for parents' planning and provision.)

We recognise that wet and windy weather can make it difficult for some children to be outdoors. Appropriate clothing provision is a very important part of supporting our view that all children can benefit from the school's outdoor learning programme. No child should be excluded from these activities because of poor clothing.

Parents are expected to send their children in appropriate seasonal clothing when requested for school activities.

Parents are notified directly about what and when to provide it, either by school newsletter or direct correspondence. The information is also available on the school website.

Some emergency spare clothing is available in Reception for Early Years children.

Tools & Resources

The designated teacher maintains an up-to-date list of the outdoor learning resources, including gardening tools, field work kit and seasonal clothing. This allows the school to plan for new and replacement acquisitions as appropriate.

Maintenance and housing of the above resources is included in this responsibility.

Use of the above resources is organised and overseen by the HOL.

(See Appendix A: List of Outdoor Learning Tools & Equipment.)

Health and Safety

Guidance is taken from County Council Guidelines for appropriate teacher/pupil ratios regarding outdoor learning activities, both on and off-site. As the risk element in certain activities increases, so the teacher/pupil ratio will need to be higher. The final ratio after risk assessment will depend on a number of factors:

- The age, sex and ability of the pupils
- The number of pupils involved
- Pupils with special educational or medical needs
- Children's previous outdoor learning experience of the activities involved
- The degree of responsibility and discipline shown by the group
- The nature of the activities involved
- The amount of risk
- The location
- The time of year
- The experience and quality of the supervisory staff
- First aid cover.

(For details of risk assessment, accident procedures, 'checking the grounds' procedure, rules for safety and behaviour management. See Appendix D: School Health & Safety Policy)

Equality and Inclusion

It is the school's responsibility to ensure all children are able to participate in the outdoor learning programme in the school grounds to the best of their ability and without undue barriers to their inclusion.

(See Appendix E: School Equal Opportunities Policy)

Off Site Visits

This policy refers specifically to outdoor learning activities based in the school grounds.

(See Appendix F: School Off-Site School Visits)

List of Appendices

(Include here an appropriate list of supporting policy documents)

A: List of Outdoor Learning Tools & Equipment

B: School Assessment & Evaluation Policy

C: School Development Plan

D: School Health & Safety Policy

E: School Equal Opportunities Policy

F: School Off-Site School Visits

Appendix 2.

Outdoor Classrooms: A Growing Convention

There has been an increasing interest in outdoor learning over the last few years. This has been largely as a result of a growing, research based awareness that children's overall learning and personal/social development benefits greatly from learning about and with nature in continuous and progressive ways.

The 'outdoor classroom' has been promoted as a way in which schools can positively support outdoor learning. Often however, companies have convinced schools that an outdoor classroom is a version of the (freestanding) pergola found in hotels, clubs, parks and gardens.

In their standard form they provide a roof for protection from the rain and some form of seating for a class of children.

Optional additions may include a sealed floor, walls, storage and access paths. The 'outdoor' nature of the space is usually maintained by having open or semi-open walls as well as its general positioning.

As with most forms of building development there is a tendency to solve the problems which are discovered through use and resulting experience, by more building. Muddy paths, trampled plants and sensitive areas, cold prevailing winds, maintenance issues, (mowing etc.) difficulties of carrying and transporting study equipment all tend to be solved by typical landscaping solutions: formal paths, walls, fencing, classroom storage etc.

If these issues are not solved, the general use and effectiveness of the outdoor classroom will decrease. Head teachers often have to re-enthuse staff to make use of what was a considerable investment. On the other hand, by over-building, the outdoor classroom increasingly loses its sense of the outdoors.

The Natural Outdoor Classroom

Outdoor learning is far better served by a simpler solution, enabling valuable resources to be used in the actual teaching and learning. In this format we are making a *social/learning investment* more than a financial one.

The most valuable part of an outdoor classroom is the *outdoors* itself – the actual area which is being visited and explored. An 'outdoor classroom' is not a room; it is nature. The more natural this area is and the more vibrant, the better. The actual class gathering space should be an integral part of this natural area in as simple a way as possible; otherwise we distance the children further from the experience we are trying to deliver.

The most integrated 'gathering space' is based on the *camp model.*

It is low impact on the environment, encouraging much greater focus on the natural area itself, both for developing its biodiversity and for the children's learning:

> It evokes an atmosphere of exploration and engagement, stimulating a real sense of interest and enthusiasm in the children.

> It is flexible, allowing for change according to seasonal or annual use.

It is much more cost effective in terms of initial outlay and continuing maintenance.

Typically such camps are small, seated areas, within or under trees, but you can create a 'camp' feel easily, no matter what you have available in your school grounds.

There are opportunities to enhance the educational potential even in something so simple. These depend primarily on the site – the fall of the land, surrounding trees/woodland and its aspect/outlook.

The fall of the land where the camp is to be sited is important for drainage and for the sense of place. If it is flat it creates a sense of being settled and 'at home' – important for the children. It should however, drain easily away from the centre and not create pools or muddiness where there is either walking or seating. This may mean initial landscape preparation before setting up the site.

Long logs are more flexible for the seating, allowing the size of the class to change but upright logs work very well too.

A central fire-pit is always recommended. Firewood is best brought in to a small site.

Additional planting is advised to enhance the natural features of the site, to ensure its sustainability and to maximise abundance of loose materials – sticks, cones, leaves, fruits etc.

For protection against weather and to create a real 'camp' feeling a simple tarpaulin canopy can be erected, either as a permanent feature or seasonally. Both work very well, but their erection will depend on whether there are surrounding trees to use as supports or whether free-standing natural supports will need to be put up.

Some fencing for security on school boundaries may need to be included in the design.

Other ways to make the 'camp' model work successfully as an outdoor learning classroom are:

To create an easily pulled, study trolley which has all the study tools needed for the subject involved. This eliminates the largest impediment to successful outdoor work teachers find – organising, distributing and keeping dry paper, books, study materials, pens and pencils and so on.

Make sure first aid, mobiles etc. are easily managed – either as part of the trolley or even in a dedicated, lock up in the outdoor site.

Design for emergency access from the beginning.

Have a tree surgeon check for weak and rotten limbs in any on-site trees.

Consider what would happen if we changed the mowing and sweeping/spraying programmes in our schools for several seasons. Nature would begin to take back the landscape. Flora and fauna would increase in number and in diversity – children would be happier and the diversity of their activity and accompanying personal development would also increase. We can 'use' this tendency to good effect by choosing where we want wilder areas and where we want more cultivates areas.

There are many simple and easy ways to build/grow the natural elements in your school grounds. Having a more natural area will enhance children's outdoor learning experiences.

Online Research Sources

Children & Nature Network - Volumes 1-5 of research documents – This site provides the most up-to-date lists and extracts of current research. It offers a huge resource of 100s of papers.
http://www.childrenandnature.org/documents/C118/

Council for Learning Outside the Classroom - A large UK site with case studies, current and archived research papers. Excellent resource.
http://www.lotc.org.uk/category/research/

Institute for Outdoor Learning
http://79.170.40.34/outdoor-learning.org/what_is_outdoor_learning/ol_research_sources.htm

English Outdoor Council
http://www.englishoutdoorcouncil.org/publications

Field Studies Council - NFER Research Review
http://www.field-studies-council.org/documents/general/NFER/NFER%20Exec%20Summary.pdf

Publications & Research Documents

Bath & North East Somerset Council: Jon Attwood (2010) *Exploring the Benefits of a Forest School Project in Twerton, Bath*
http://www.bathnes.gov.uk/SiteCollectionDocuments/Education%20and%20Learning/Forest%20School%20Final%20Report%20-%20Twerton%20Summer%202010.pdf

BCEP - Bradford Community Environment Project: Lily Horseman (2010) *Reflections and Evaluation on Forest School projects 2010*
http://www.bradfordforestschools.co.uk/siteFiles/ReflectionsAndEvaluation.pdf

Chawla, Louise (2001) *Significant Life Experiences Revisited Once Again: response to Vol. 5(4) 'Five Critical Commentaries on Significant Life Experience Research in Environmental Education'* Environmental Education Research, 7: 4, 451 — 461

DEFRA - The Department for Environment, Food and Rural Affairs (2012) *The Natural Choice – Securing The Value Of Nature*

Dimensions Educational Research Foundation: Vicki Bohling, Cindy Saarela, Dana Miller (2011) *How Can Something This Good Be So Simple - Supporting Parent Engagement in Children's Learning Outdoors*
http://www.dimensionsfoundation.org/research/documents/ParentSupportForestLkMN_11.pdf

Education Scotland: *Outdoor Learning - Practical guidance, ideas and support for teachers and practitioners in Scotland*
http://www.educationscotland.gov.uk/resources/o/outdoorlearningpracticalguidanceideasandsupportforteachersandpractitionersinscotland.asp

English Outdoor Council: Randall Williams – Chair (2010) *Time For Change in Outdoor Learning - Hard evidence on the value of the outdoors and a challenge to deliver fair access for all*
http://www.outdoorindustriesassociation.co.uk/cust_images/Change.pdf

FACE - Farming & Countryside Education: Dr Aric Sigman (2007) *Agricultural Literacy – Giving Concrete Children Food For Thought*
http://www.face-online.org.uk/resources/news/Agricultural%20Literacy.pdf

Forestry Commission England: Liz O'Brien and Richard Murray (2006) *A marvellous opportunity for children to learn - A participatory evaluation of Forest School in England and Wales* http://www.forestry.gov.uk/pdf/fr0112forestschoolsreport.pdf/$FILE/fr0112forestschoolsreport.pdf

Kenny, Rowena - Bath Spa University (2010) *A Critical Exploration of the Role of 'Resilience' in Relation to the Learning and Development of Young Children*
http://bathspa.academia.edu/RowenaKenny/Papers/540221/A_critical_exploration_of_the_role_of_the_learning_disposition_resilience_in_the_learning_and_development_of_young_children

Kenny, Rowena - Bath Spa University (2010) *A critical review of research and literature exploring the relationship of the child with the natural world*
http://bathspa.academia.edu/RowenaKenny/Papers/540222/A_critical_review_of_research_and_literature_exploring_the_relationship_of_the_child_with_the_natural_world

Kenny, Rowena - Bath Spa University (2010) *Involve, Enjoy, Achieve: Forest School and the Early Years Foundation Stage – An Exploratory Case Study*
http://bathspa.academia.edu/RowenaKenny/Papers/677644/Forest_School_and_the_Early_Years_Foundation_Stage_-_An_Exploratory_Case_Study

Learning Through Landscapes: *Shared Visions and Values for Outdoor Play*
http://www.ltl.org.uk/Contribute/PDF/VisionandValues.pdf

Louv, R. (2005) *Last Child in the Woods: Saving Our Children from Nature Deficit Disorder*. New York: Algonquin Books

NCB - National Children's Bureau: Rachel Blades, Chloe Gill (2010) *Evaluation of Play England – A Summary of Years One to Four*
http://www.ncb.org.uk/media/443987/summary_of_the_play_england_evaluation-_years_1-4.pdf

NFER - National Foundation For Educational Research & King's College London: Mark Rickinson, Justin Dillon, Kelly Teamey, Marian Morris, Mee Young Choi, Dawn Sanders, Pauline Benefield (2004) *Review of Research on Outdoor Learning*
http://www.field-studies-council.org/documents/general/NFER/A_review_of_research_on_outdoor_learning.pdf

NFER: Justin Dillon, Marian Morris, Lisa O'Donnell, Alan Reid, Mark Rickinson, William Scott (2005) *Engaging and Learning with the Outdoors – The Final Report of the Outdoor Classroom in a Rural Context Action Research Project*
http://www.bath.ac.uk/cree/resources/OCR.pdf

(The) National Environmental Education & Training Foundation (2000) *Environment-based Education – creating high performance schools and students*
http://www.neefusa.org/pdf/NEETF8400.pdf

National Trust (UK) Stephen Moss (2012) *Natural Childhood*
http://www.nationaltrust.org.uk/servlet/file/store5/item823323/version1/Natural%20Childhood%20Brochure.pdf

Natural England Commissioned Report NECR092: DILLON, J. & DICKIE, I. (2012) *Learning in the Natural Environment: Review of social and economic benefits and barriers*
http://publications.naturalengland.org.uk/publication/1321181

Natural England Commissioned Report NECR097: Mark Rickinson, Anne Hunt, Jim Rogers, Justin Dillon (2012) *School Leader and Teacher Insights into Learning Outside the Classroom in Natural Environments - A Study to Inform the Natural Connections Demonstration Project*
http://www.lotc.org.uk/wp-content/uploads/2012/08/School-Leader-Teacher-insight.pdf

Outdoor Education Advisers' Panel: (2011) *Research Supporting Outdoor Learning, Offsite Visits and LOtC*
http://oeapng.info/wp-content/uploads/downloads/2012/04/2.4c-Research-Supporting-Outdoor-Learning-and-LOtC-Final-1.pdf

Palmer, Sue (2006) *Toxic Childhood – How The Modern World Is Damaging Our Children And What We Can Do About It.* London: Orion Books

Palmer, Sue (2010) *21st Century Boys: How Modern Life Can Drive Them off the Rails and How to Get Them Back on Track.* London: Orion Books

Robinson, Ken (2010) *The Element: How Finding Your Passion Changes Everything.* Chichester: Capstone Publishing

Robinson, Ken (2011) *Out Of Our Minds – Learning To Be Creative.* Penguin

Sobel, David (2008) *Childhood And Nature – Design Principles For Educators.* Stenhouse Publishers

Social and Economic Research Group, Forest Research: Liz O'Brien and Rebecca Lovell (2011) *A review of the Forest Education Initiative in Britain*
http://www.forestry.gov.uk/pdf/FEI_review_2011.pdf/$file/FEI_review_2011.pdf

The New Economics Foundation, NEF: Richard Murray (2003) *Forest School Evaluation Project - A Study in Wales, April to November, 2003*
http://www.forestry.gov.uk/pdf/ForestSchoolWalesReport.pdf/$FILE/ForestSchoolWalesReport.pdf

The University of Cambridge: Dir. Robin Alexander (2009) *The Cambridge Primary Review*
http://www.primaryreview.org.uk/Downloads/Finalreport/CPR-booklet_low-res.pdf

University of Plymouth: Bernie Davis and Sue Waite (2005) *Forest Schools: An Evaluation of the Opportunities and Challenges in Early Years. Final Report*
http://books.google.co.uk/books/about/Forest_Schools.html?id=kzmNYgEACAAJ&redir_esc=y

Printed in Germany
by Amazon Distribution
GmbH, Leipzig